Dear Reader,

One of the best things about being a romance writer is the ability to travel—in my mind. When I really need a vacation, I choose a setting that appeals to me and start to write.

As I write this, it's the middle of winter here in Wisconsin. The weather bounces between brutal (-30 windchills) to balmy (above-freezing days). I woke this morning to more snow. But later today, I'll be comfortably sitting in July humidity on a veranda in a small North Carolina town. It almost makes winter bearable.

I hope you enjoy the next installment in the Mighty Quinns series. By the time this hits the shelves, it will be summer in Wisconsin and I'll probably be writing a book set in the middle of a snowstorm!

Happy reading,

Kate Hoffmann

Kate Hoffmann

The Mighty Quinns: Devin

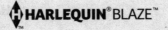

HARLEQUIN® BLAZE™

Recycling programs
for this product may
not exist in your area.

ISBN-13: 978-0-373-79860-5

The Mighty Quinns: Devin

Copyright © 2015 by Peggy A. Hoffmann

Printed in U.S.A.

Kate Hoffmann celebrated her twentieth anniversary as a Harlequin author in August 2013. She has published over eighty books, novellas and short stories for Harlequin Temptation and Harlequin Blaze. She spent time as a music teacher, a retail assistant and an advertising exec before she settled into a career as a full-time writer. Her other interests include genealogy, musical theater and vegan cooking. She lives in southeastern Wisconsin with her two cats, Winnie and Gracie.

Books by Kate Hoffmann

HARLEQUIN BLAZE

The Mighty Quinns

The Mighty Quinns: Kellan
The Mighty Quinns: Dermot
The Mighty Quinns: Kieran
The Mighty Quinns: Cameron
The Mighty Quinns: Ronan
The Mighty Quinns: Logan
The Mighty Quinns: Jack
The Mighty Quinns: Rourke
The Mighty Quinns: Dex
The Mighty Quinns: Malcolm
The Mighty Quinns: Rogan
The Mighty Quinns: Ryan
The Mighty Quinns: Eli

To get the inside scoop on Harlequin Blaze and its talented writers, be sure to check out blazeauthors.com.

All backlist available in ebook format.

Visit the Author Profile page at Harlequin.com for more titles.

Prologue

"STAND UP STRAIGHT, don't chew with your mouth open, and say 'thank you' when they give you your gift."

Devin Cassidy glanced over at his mother as they strode down the icy sidewalk. Mary Cassidy's gaze was fixed in front of her, her lips pressed into a hard line. She'd worked as a housekeeper for the powerful Winchester family for as long as Dev could remember and she took her position in the household very seriously.

Every morning except for Sundays, she'd leave the house before sunrise, dressed in a simple gray uniform, and return an hour before he went to bed. She was usually too exhausted to do more than acknowledge his existence before flopping down onto the sofa in the corner of the living room with a glass of whiskey and cool washcloth for her head. Dev would prepare supper for her and place it on a tray table next to the sofa, then turn on the television before retreating to his tiny bedroom.

When he was younger, he'd wondered why he didn't have a normal family as many of his friends did—a father, a mother, a few siblings, even a pair of grandparents. But when he'd questioned his mother, his inquiries had always been met with stony silence. "I'm your mother," she'd say. "I provide for you. You won't need anyone else in the world."

He didn't ask anymore. He'd lived without a father for this long. They didn't need some undependable guy walking into their lives and turning everything upside down. They got by fine just the two of them.

By the time they reached the Winchester mansion, his feet and fingers were numb with cold and his nose was running. His mother examined his appearance carefully, wiping his nose with her lace-edged handkerchief and smoothing his ruffled hair with her fingers. "The Winchesters believe children should be seen and not heard," she reminded him.

"I'm not a child," he muttered. Hell, he was nearly thirteen years old and he'd been making this same walk to the Winchesters every Christmas since he could remember. But his attitude about the party at the end of the walk had changed.

Used to be that the prospect of getting an expensive gift was all he could think about. There had never been much money for Santa, so the Winchester gift always made up for it. On top of that, there was food—all sorts of treats that he'd never tasted. And he got to gaze at the beautiful Christmas tree that soared to the ceiling in the front parlor, and indulge in cups of punch that tasted like fizzy sherbet.

The Winchesters were different…special. Everyone knew they were rich, but with all that money came respect and undeniable power. One did not speak badly of the Winchesters. In fact, everyone in town was beholden to them.

Frederick Winchester owned the town—he owned the huge textile mill that sat on the river, most of the businesses in the quaint downtown, many of the smaller homes that lined the quiet streets. If the family didn't like someone, it became impossible for him to live in Winchester.

Without her job in the Winchester mansion, Dev's mother had nothing. They paid rent on their little house directly to Frederick Winchester, they bought things on credit at the grocers—also owned by Winchester—and when someone was sick, they went to the Winchester Clinic.

Dev stood behind his mother as she rapped sharply on the ornately carved front door. A few moments later, one of the Winchester children opened the front door. There were no servants on duty that night. For one night a year, the family would wait on their staff.

It was a Christmas tradition, but even with the forced gaiety, it made for an uncomfortable evening. At no other time were the stark differences between the "haves" and the "have-nots" clearer.

"Good evening," the young girl said.

"Good evening, Miss Elodie," his mother replied. "You look lovely tonight."

"Thank you, Mary. So do you." She stepped aside, and Dev and his mother walked into the wide entry hall. Elodie turned to Dev and held out her hand. "Hello, Devin. It's nice to see you again. May I take your coats?"

Dev stared at her hand for a long moment, then gave it a quick shake. "Thanks," he muttered. He slipped out of his jacket and waited as his mother handed the girl her coat, as well. Elodie disappeared for a moment, then returned without the coats.

"Let me take you in," she said, leading them toward the huge parlor to the right of the sweeping stairway. Dev kept his eyes fixed on Elodie. He remembered her from Christmases past, but she'd grown up over the past year. She wasn't a little girl anymore but a confident young lady, tall and graceful and—pretty.

"Mama, Papa, look who's here. Mary and her son, Devin."

The entire family surrounded them, offering Mary their holiday greetings. Dev did as was expected of him. He shook their hands and made his greetings. When the family pointed to the tables loaded with food, Dev politely chose some treats, then found a quiet place to sit near the butler's pantry. There were other children at the party, but they'd also been warned to mind their manners and they were sitting quietly, enjoying the cakes and candies near the Christmas tree.

The grand finale of the party would be the gift-giving, the part that Dev hated most of all. Frederick Winchester would present each of the children with an extravagant gift and then would wait for each of his employees to express their deepest gratitude to Winchester for giving them the job that fed their families and put a roof over their heads.

Of course, there were tears and long descriptions of the kindness that the Winchesters showed their inferiors. Dev had to wonder how his mother did it, year after year, never questioning her place in their world, never quibbling over her meager pay or her long work hours.

Dev wondered how much longer *he'd* be able to pretend that this was all right with him. Last year, he'd refused to open the gift he'd been given—a brand-new PlayStation, he'd discovered when he'd opened it later that night. He didn't have the money to buy the games, but then, Frederick Winchester wouldn't have considered that.

He'd taken the gift out to the garage the day after Christmas and smashed it to pieces with a hammer. And when his mother had asked where it was, he'd told her that he'd donated it to the toy drive at school.

Dev hated having to bow and scrape to the Winchesters just because they were rich. But this job was important to his mother, and for her, Dev would do anything. It was the only thing that stood between them and poverty. Someday, he'd have an important job that paid well and they'd be able to walk away from Winchesters and their money.

"Psst."

Dev looked up from his plate and noticed a small opening in the door to the butler's pantry. The door opened a bit farther and he recognized Elodie's face.

"What?" Dev asked.

"You want to see something?" she asked.

He glanced around, but no one was paying any attention to him sitting alone in the corner of the room. "What?"

The door opened a little farther. "Come, I'll show you," she said.

Dev set his plate down on a nearby table, then quietly slipped from the room. When he got inside the dark butler's pantry, her hand gripped his, and he followed after her as they ran through the kitchen to the servants' stairway. He'd been in the house a number of times over the years with his mother, but he'd never ventured upstairs.

"Are you sure we should be up here?" he asked.

"Of course, silly. This is my house. I can go anywhere I want."

They seemed to climb stairs forever, the last flight narrow and twisting. Finally, Elodie threw open a door and turned on the lights.

"Where are we?" he asked.

"A secret room," she said. "In the attic."

"What's up here?"

"Come and see," she said, drawing him inside.

The wide room was dominated by a huge table, but it was impossible to distinguish what was on top, as the contents were covered with a sheet. And then, suddenly, Elodie ripped off the sheet and flipped a switch. The table lit up and toy trains began to circle a series of winding tracks.

Dev stepped closer, fascinated by the sight. There had to be at least ten trains, all winding their way through a number of trestles and tunnels and passing through towns with tiny houses all lit up from the inside. Miniature cars sat at the crossings, waiting for the gates to rise when the trains passed.

"Holy shit," Dev muttered.

"Yeah. Holy shit," Elodie repeated.

He glanced over at her and laughed. "Is this yours?"

She shook her head. "No, it belonged to my grandfather. When he was alive, he used to let us play with it every Christmas, but now my father keeps the door locked."

"How did you get in?"

"I know where the key is," she said. "I sneak up here all the time. I just have to remember exactly where the trains were when I started and I put them back before I leave."

"Why won't your father let you play with it?"

"He hates these trains. He and my grandfather never really got along. I miss him."

"Where is he?"

"He died when I was seven," she said. "He was living in California with my aunt Charlotte."

"I'm sorry," Dev said, surprised to see tears in her eyes. He reached out and took her hand, giving it a squeeze.

"Me, too," she said. "I'm sure my grandfather would want me to play with the trains, though. It always made him laugh."

Elodie showed him the controls and watched as he operated the trains by himself. She walked around the table, pointing out all her favorite train cars and buildings. He set the controls down and followed her, listening to her voice, caught up in the magic of the moment.

And then, it was over. She glanced at her watch and

cried out. "It's time for the gifts," she said, hurrying to the door. "Come on, we have to get back."

"Don't you have to fix the trains?"

"I'll sneak up later," she said, flinging the sheet over the table.

They rushed down the three flights, then hurried through the kitchen to the butler's pantry. Elodie peeked through the door. "You go first. If they ask where you were, just tell them that I helped you find the bathroom."

Dev turned to face her, then, taking a chance, he leaned toward her and kissed her cheek. He'd never kissed a girl before and was surprised at how easy— and enjoyable—it was. "Thanks," he said. "I had fun."

Elodie smiled. "Me, too."

As he stepped back into the dining room, Dev realized that he'd never think of the Winchesters' Christmas party the same way again. He'd always remember this night and the moment he kissed Elodie Winchester on the cheek.

When it came time for the gifts, she was the one who handed him his elaborately wrapped present.

"I picked it out especially for you," she whispered.

Dev smiled.

He watched her for the rest of the night as she mingled among the guests. If he could have kissed her again, he would have. But he knew the dangers of crossing that invisible line. As much as he might enjoy Elodie's company, this was just one night.

It all would begin and end right here.

1

DEV CASSIDY PULLED the police cruiser up to the curb in front of Zelda's Café and turned off the ignition. The sun had come up over an hour ago and the sleepy town of Winchester was just beginning to move.

When the mill had been operating, the town's days had begun much earlier, the blare of the first-shift whistle splitting the morning silence at precisely 6:00 a.m. But everything had changed since the Winchester family's flagship business had failed. A secure future had disappeared for so many of the town's residents. Stores had closed, people had moved out, more businesses had closed, and within three years Winchester was nothing but a shell filled with empty buildings and broken lives.

Most everyone blamed Frederick Winchester, but Dev knew it had been a confluence of events. The Winchester textile mill had been one of the last independently owned family mills in the state. Competing with the newer, more state-of-the-art corporate mills had been an impossible task. The national financial collapse of 2008 hadn't helped.

Still, the whole thing had left behind a bitter taste for the residents of Winchester. A few weeks after closing the mill, the family had packed up and moved out of town. Then the truth had come out. The Winchesters were bankrupt, the mill mortgaged to the hilt, and there was nothing left to do but close and liquidate. Pensions had disappeared and hopes and dreams of a bright future had been dashed.

It might not have been so bad if it hadn't been for the way Frederick had handled the situation. With no interest in trying to salvage the business, he'd held a fire sale. Within a week, they'd buried their father and left with the last pennies of the family fortune. All that remained was the mansion that sat on the hill overlooking what was left of Winchester.

As Dev got out of the car, he glanced up at the freshly painted sign above the café's door. Zelda's Café had opened last month, spurred on by the town council's attempt to rejuvenate the downtown. The owner, Joan Fitzgerald, had been a manager at the mill and was now baking her prize-winning cinnamon rolls and serving up fancy coffee drinks with exotic Italian names.

The bell above the door jingled as he stepped inside the cool interior. Air-conditioning was always a pleasant relief from the hot, humid weather that was typical for early July in the Blue Ridge Mountains. Dev took a spot at the counter and grabbed a menu, checking out the specials before settling on his usual.

Joanie approached with a mug and the coffeepot.

"Gonna be a hot one today. You sure I can't get you a sweet tea instead of coffee?"

"Hit me with the caffeine," he said, nodding to the mug. "And I'll have my usual."

"Grannie's Granola with yogurt and berries," she said. "Raspberries today. I picked them fresh yesterday."

He watched her prepare the dish, layering her homemade granola with fresh vanilla yogurt in a parfait glass. She topped it with a handful of berries and set it in front of him.

The place was still quiet, so Joanie pulled up a stool and sat across from him, sipping at a glass of orange juice. "That break-in down at Feller's filling station? You might want to talk to Jimmy Joe Babcock about that. His brother was in here yesterday and mentioned a brand-new set of tires he received from Jimmy Joe for his birthday."

Zelda's was the central processing station for most of the town's gossip, now that the mill was closed. If there was anything of interest going on in Winchester, Joanie heard about it and passed it along to Dev. Like a few other local businesspeople in town, she understood that if Winchester was going to flourish again, Dev needed to rid it of the petty crime that chipped away at its foundation.

"Yeah, I had my eye on him. That boy needs a job. Sixteen and already in big trouble. Can't you find a spot for him here at the restaurant?"

Joanie shook her head. "I'm already overstaffed with dishwashers and bussers, thanks to you. Now, if he could wash windows, I might have work for him."

Dev looked over at the café's huge plate-glass windows that faced the street. "I could probably help you out with that," he said.

He chatted with a few of the customers as he finished his breakfast, then grabbed another coffee to go before he waved goodbye to Joanie. "I'll send someone by to get at those windows," he called as he walked out the door.

Dev stood outside the café and took in the street, his gaze drifting from one end to the other. Most of the buildings were empty, windows revealing one failure after another. But here and there, small entrepreneurs had found a way to make something new. Winchester had always depended upon the mill for its livelihood, and now the town needed something different. But what?

Dev fixed his gaze on a white sedan he didn't recognize at the far end of the block. He watched as it slowly drove by. Rental plates. He looked up at the driver and his breath caught in his throat. Their eyes locked for a moment and his pulse leaped. Elodie Winchester?

She was there in front of him and then just as quickly disappearing down the road. He glanced down at the car's license plate and quickly memorized the number. When he got to the cruiser, he grabbed the radio and called in to dispatch. "Sally, this is Dev. I need you to run a plate for me. It's a rental car, probably out of Asheville." Dev recited the numbers and then sat back and waited for Sally's results, sipping his coffee as his mind spun with the possibilities.

It didn't make sense. The Winchester family had

cleared out six years ago. And after the mess they'd left, most folks didn't expect to see a real Winchester ever again—and didn't want to.

Hell, maybe he was just imagining the whole thing. Would he even recognize Elodie? They'd spent a single summer together. He'd been seventeen, she'd been sixteen, and they'd been madly in love.

Her family never would have approved, so they'd sneaked around, meeting on the sly, stealing kisses whenever they could and pledging their love to each other in silly teenage sentiments. Of course, they'd been found out, but neither one of them could have predicted the devastating repercussions.

Without warning, Elodie's bags had been packed and she was sent away. She no longer attended the private girls' school an hour away in Asheville. She wouldn't be home every evening for dinner and wouldn't be able to sneak out and meet him once the sun set. There would be no long lazy summers at the lake or cozy winters sitting by a campfire. It was over.

There'd been a lot of women since Elodie. He'd forgotten most of them, but Elodie Winchester had stuck with him. Maybe it was because they'd never had any kind of closure. She'd never called, never written. When she'd come home for Christmas holidays, she'd been invisible.

Dev hadn't tried to contact her. Frederick Winchester had made it clear that if Dev tried to contact Elodie, Mary Cassidy would find herself without a job, without a home to live in, and without any prospects for finding work in Winchester in the future. So he'd let her go. At least, on the surface.

"Dispatch to RC zero-one." A blast of static followed and Dev reached for the radio.

"This is Dev. What do you have for me, Sally?"

"You were right. That rental came out of Acme Rentals in Asheville."

"Who rented the car?"

"Elodie Winchester," Sally said. "She's got it for a week."

Dev let out a tightly held breath, sinking back into his seat. "Thanks, Sally. Keep this to yourself, all right?"

"Sure, boss. What do you think she's doing in town again?"

"I don't know."

"Will there be trouble?"

"People haven't forgotten what the Winchesters did to this place. But Elodie had no part in that. She shouldn't be blamed."

"She's a Winchester," Sally said. "That puts a big target on her back."

"Yes, it does," he murmured. "I'll pay her a visit later, make sure everything's okay. Call me if you hear anything else. Meantime, I'm going to head over to the high school. I need to have a conversation with Jimmy Joe Babcock."

"Ten-four, boss."

He started the cruiser and steered it toward the high school, his mind still mulling over the reality of seeing Elodie again.

He'd always wondered what kind of woman she'd become. As a teenager, she'd been sweet and silly, far too naive and willing to love unconditionally. She'd softened his rough edges, made him believe that he could be something, do something with his life. She'd always seen the best in people and refused to believe the worst, even when the truth slapped her in the face.

Dev had been the opposite. By the time he was seventeen, he'd amassed a rather sizable chip on his shoulder. He'd witnessed firsthand how the town and the Winchesters could wear a person down. He had just one plan, and that was to get as far away as fast as he could. And he'd done just that, leaving the day after his high school graduation.

He'd worked odd jobs and put himself through school, getting a criminal justice degree in five years. He'd all set to enter the police academy in Atlanta when his mother called. The Winchesters were bankrupt, she was about to lose her job and her home, and she had no idea what to do.

Dev had returned to Winchester within the month and had been lucky enough to sign on with the local police department as a rookie patrolman. As the town economy worsened over the next five years, many of his fellow officers moved on to better jobs. And two years ago, he'd been the senior officer in the department and accepted the job of police chief—at a greatly reduced salary from the last police chief.

But Dev liked his job. He knew what he was doing was important. If the town had any chance of bouncing back, it would happen only if he could keep crime at bay. A single meth lab, a car theft ring, even a clever burglar, could bring it all crashing down. Once the town had a reputation for trouble, no one would want to live there or visit and the town would never recover.

His attention focused on a small group of smokers, huddled near the edge of the school parking lot. Dev threw the car into gear and slowly pulled up in front of them. "You boys really want to spend the rest of your life buying cigarettes? You get hooked now, it's much harder to kick it later. It's an expensive habit." Dev turned and grinned at Jimmy Joe. "And where are you getting money for smokes, Babcock? After spending all that cash on those tires for your brother, I'd think you'd be broke right about now."

Dev got out of the car and stepped in front of Babcock. "The rest of you can check your homework. I need to have a word with Jimmy Joe." The boys exchanged glances and the group slowly broke up.

When they were alone and the others were out of earshot, Dev leaned back against the cruiser and crossed his arms over his chest. "I know you stole those tires from Feller's. The only thing I don't know is what you plan to do about it."

Jimmy Joe stared down at the ground. "What can I do? I can't give them back. My brother already put them on his car."

"I'm sure if you offered to pay for them, we could work something out."

"I don't have any money," Jimmy Joe said.

"Not now. But if you find yourself a job, you'll have some cash."

"There are no jobs," he said. "My dad's been looking for two years."

"You really want to fix this?" Dev asked.

Jimmy Joe nodded.

"After school, you walk over to the hardware store. I'm going to leave a list of supplies for you to pick up. You can pay for them on my account. Then I want you to bring everything over to Zelda's. I'll meet you there."

"What are we going to do?"

"We're going to turn you into an upstanding citizen of Winchester," Dev said. "And until you pay Marv back for those tires, I don't want to see you spending money on cigarettes."

"Yes, sir."

"Now, get to class. No more trouble."

Dev watched the kid walk away.

One by one, he'd deal with the problems in Winchester. It was all he could do. Lately it seemed he was scrambling just to keep ahead of the game instead of doing anything proactive. But if Jimmy Joe showed up at Zelda's, he could count his day a success.

Dev got back into the cruiser. Now he needed to address another problem. But this problem promised to be more personal than professional.

ELODIE WINCHESTER SLOWLY climbed the porch steps of her childhood home. Somewhere in the distance, a blue jay's call echoed in the quiet morning breeze. She reached out and ran her hand along the painted rail, now weathered with age and peeling with neglect.

Made of the local red brick, the house was a sprawling homage to the Queen Anne style. A wide veranda circled the entire first floor, interspersed with simple wooden columns that held up a shingled roof. It had been built by her great-grandfather at the turn of the century, completed just ten years after he opened his textile mill.

But the house had been empty for six years and she could see the work that would be required to bring it back to its former glory.

Elodie had never really looked at the house from a maintenance viewpoint. To her, it had always been more like a fairy castle, with its high-peaked roofs and rooftop widow's walk. Now it was her house, the only compensation she'd received after her father had raided her trust fund in a futile attempt to save his failing investments.

All of her siblings had suffered the same fate, but most of them had already been drawing on their trusts for years. She'd had the most to lose, so she'd gotten the only thing left that hadn't—or couldn't—be sold.

The house had been on the market for years, but its deteriorating condition and the floundering town had driven away all the qualified buyers. No one in Winchester could afford to buy it, much less live in it. And no one from out of town wanted to live here.

She pulled the keys out of her pocket and opened the front door, letting it swing wide before she stepped across the threshold. To her surprise, the house didn't smell musty. Although the air was hot and stuffy, the scent of lemon oil and floor wax lingered in the air.

As Elodie strolled through the nearly empty rooms,

she ran her finger over chair rails and mantels, finding barely a trace of dust. The sound of running water startled her and she followed it to the back of the house where the kitchen was located. A slender figure, dressed in a familiar gray uniform, stood over the sink.

"Mary?" Elodie said. "Mary Cassidy?"

The woman turned, a bucket clutched in her hand. "Miss Elodie. I heard you were back in town. The minute I did, I came right over. The place is a bit dusty, but I'll have it sparkling again in no time."

"Mary, I don't understand. Have you been cleaning here all along?"

She nodded. "I just couldn't let it all go to ruin," Mary said. "I come once a week and do what I can. I have to say, it's much easier without all the furniture."

"Who is paying you?"

"Oh, no one. I don't need to be paid. I just want the house to look presentable. For you and the rest of the family."

Elodie stared at the woman in disbelief. The family had left six years ago and they'd closed the house a few months later. "I—I don't know how to thank you," she murmured.

"Are you planning to stay here?" Mary asked. "If you are, I'll go up and get your room ready. Most of the furniture is still there. We'll need to get the electricity turned on, but the plumbing works just fine. And with this weather, you won't need heat."

"Mary, it's not necessary for you to— I mean, I can't pay you a lot. I don't have much left."

"Oh, don't you worry about that, Miss Elodie. I'm

sure we'll sort it all out later. Now, if you'll excuse me, I'm just going to get to work on your bedroom."

"Thank you, Mary."

Elodie watched as the woman hurried off. An image of Dev flashed in her mind, and she sucked in a sharp breath. Twice now, she'd been reminded of him. Earlier this morning, when she'd seen a man who resembled him, and now, coming face-to-face with Devin's mother.

Her thoughts returned to the policeman. Maybe she'd just been hoping that he'd still be in Winchester. Elodie knew the odds were against it. He'd always wanted to leave. And why would Dev stay? There was nothing for him here, especially now that the jobs had dried up. And she hadn't really seen the guy's face. He'd worn sunglasses and a baseball cap pulled low over his eyes.

But there had been something familiar about the man's mouth, she mused. It reminded her of that crooked smile of Dev's that she remembered so well.

Drawing a deep breath, she started out of the kitchen, then stopped short.

There he was. Dressed in navy blue, a badge hanging from a chain around his neck. But the cap and the sunglasses were gone. Elodie swallowed hard. "Hello." It was all she could manage.

"The front door was open," he said. "I thought it was you this morning."

"I thought I recognized you, too."

He grinned in that same sweet boyish way she remembered. "You haven't changed a bit," Dev murmured. "Still...beautiful."

"Devin Cassidy." Her heart slammed in her chest and

her knees trembled. This was crazy. They'd been high school sweethearts, but that had been years ago. Why was she having such a powerful reaction to seeing him again? Other than the fact he was now an absolutely gorgeous specimen of manhood. "You look…older. I mean, you look like a—a grown-up."

"Elodie," he replied with a chuckle. "Still the most honest person I've ever met."

"You're a—a policeman?"

"Chief of police, actually," he said. "What are you doing back in town?"

Elodie wasn't sure she wanted to get into the complicated details of her trip. But if she didn't continue the conversation, he might leave, and she was certain she didn't want that. In truth, she wanted a nice, long time to just stare at him, to admire the adult he'd become, to take in every little detail of his face until she'd erased the boy in her memories and replaced him with this incredibly sexy man.

"I'm here to tie up some loose ends. The house has been for sale for years and we've had no biters, so I'm considering donating it to the town or maybe to the county."

"Why would you do that?"

"I can't afford the taxes any longer. And there's maintenance that needs to be done that can't be put off. It's become an anchor around my neck."

"Instead of abandoning it, you could always stick around and make something of it."

She laughed softly. "Like what?"

"I don't know. It just seems to me that a Winchester should be living in this house."

"Well, there will be one living here for the next week or two," she said.

"You're staying here?"

"It's cheaper than a motel. I can rough it. Your mother is upstairs putting my bedroom back together." Elodie met his gaze. "Has she been coming here all along?"

Dev shrugged. "I suppose someone should have asked you, but she wasn't doing any harm. Your family was her life. She started working for your parents when she was a teenager. I think this is the closest thing she's ever had to a real home and she couldn't stand to see it neglected."

"I can't pay her," Elodie said.

"That's the last thing that matters to her," he replied.

A long silence grew between them. "I—I'd offer you a cool drink, but I haven't had a chance to shop." She laughed. "And right now, I have no electricity for the refrigerator."

His portable radio squawked. He grabbed it and clicked it on. "This is Dev," he said.

"We've got a report of a 10-68 out on Highway 16, just west of Mike Murphy's place."

"I'm five minutes away," Dev said. "I've got it. Out." He smiled at Elodie. "I have to go. Duty calls."

"I hope it's not something dangerous," she said.

"Nope. A 10-68 is livestock in roadway. I suspect one of Mike Murphy's pigs got loose. He raises particularly brilliant pigs. They always seem to figure out a way to open the gate and run onto the road rather than crawl through the big broken gaps in his fencing and into the field beyond."

Elodie laughed. "Glad to hear it's nothing dangerous. I won't have to worry." A blush warmed her cheeks. Had that been too forward? After all, they were barely more than strangers now. And yet, it didn't feel that way. He felt like an old friend, like someone she'd known very well and hadn't seen for a few years.

"All right," he said. "I have to get back to work. I'll stop by later."

"I'll be fine," she said. "Don't worry about me." Oh, now she was assuming *he* was concerned about *her*? "Not that I think you're worried," Elodie added. "You have more important things to deal with. So don't—"

He reached out and pressed his finger to her lips. The contact was startling and undeniably intimate. "You're currently residing in the village of Winchester, where I am the chief of police," he said. "It's my responsibility to worry about your well-being."

Elodie forced a smile. "All right," she said.

Dev nodded, then strode through the house to the front door. She heard it close behind him, and she sank back against the wall.

It had been twelve years since she'd last seen him and nothing had changed between them. He still had the ability to set her heart racing and turn her brain to mush. It had taken every ounce of her willpower to stop herself from touching him and running her fingers over his handsome face.

She'd met a lot of boys, and then men, since leaving Winchester. She'd had some serious relationships that had ended up imploding in a spectacular fashion. And in the midst of all that pain and turmoil, Elodie had always wondered if she'd left her one true love behind at age sixteen.

The notion was ridiculous, but it had stuck with her over the years. Maybe she'd been fated to love Devin Cassidy, and she'd never be truly happy unless she was with him. Elodie sighed. Or maybe she was searching for something—a sense of belonging, a place for her to finally feel safe and secure again. She was home, but it wasn't the home she remembered. It was silly to get too attached to Dev simply because he was familiar.

She closed her eyes and let a delicious image of the dark-haired, blue-eyed man drift through her mind. How was it possible that he was still here, still single and— Elodie stopped herself. *Was* he still single? She hadn't bothered to check for a wedding band. Surely she would have noticed that.

Elodie opened her eyes and pushed away from the wall. "Mary?" She ran through the house and took the stairs to her bedroom two at a time.

If she wanted to know more about Winchester's sexy police chief, she'd simply ask his mother.

2

"I UNDERSTAND THAT there's a procedure to turn the power back on," Dev said, "but I'm asking you to do me this favor. Come on, Jack, I'll pay the overtime or the upcharge or whatever's necessary to get your guys out there this afternoon. With all the bad feelings around town about the Winchesters, it's not safe for Elodie Winchester to stay in that house with the power off. Now, if you want that responsibility on your head, you've got it. Anything happens to her, I'll let everyone know that we talked."

Dev pushed the grocery cart up to the checkout register and began to unload the groceries as he listened to Jack's excuses on the other end of the line. He smiled at the young girl behind the register. Erv and Maggie Ronkowski's daughter. Honor student. Caroline. Played flute in the high school band.

He suddenly remembered that he was supposed to meet Jimmy Joe in front of Zelda's after school. Dev glanced at his watch. School let out ten minutes ago.

Jimmy Joe was probably at the hardware store picking up supplies. If he hurried, he'd make it on time.

"Jack, just get it done. I'll owe you one." He switched off his phone and shoved it in his pocket. "Hey there, Caroline," he said. "How's it going?"

"Good," she said. "Would you like paper or plastic?"

"Paper is fine," he said.

He waited as she called over the manager to check out the wine he'd purchased. The store manager, Eddie Grant, strolled over and began to bag the groceries. "Did you hear that one of the Winchesters is back in town?"

"I did," Dev said. "Elodie. The youngest daughter."

"Jeb Baylor was in here talkin' that he and a bunch of the boys were going to pay her a visit later. They're all upset about the pension thing and they want some answers."

"Did they define 'later'?"

"Yeah, after work. You might want to stop by and calm them down."

"I'll do that," Dev said. He held out his credit card and signed the slip before scooping up the pair of grocery bags. "Thanks, Eddie. You're a good guy."

"I remember Elodie," he said. "She used to come in here and buy candy when she was a kid. She was always really sweet."

"She still is," Dev said.

When he got to the cruiser, Dev threw the groceries in the back, then grabbed his radio. "Car zero-one to dispatch."

"Dispatch," Sally said. "What can I do for you, Chief?"

"Get Kyle on the radio and have him drive over to the Winchester mansion. There's talk of some trouble. Have him sit on the place until I get there."

"Ten-four," Sally said.

He listened as she made the call, then pulled the cruiser out into traffic. By the time he reached Zelda's, Jimmy Joe was waiting for him, his purchases scattered on the sidewalk in front of him.

Dev jumped out of the car and jogged across the street. "Nice work," he said.

"What is all this stuff?"

"Grab the bucket and take it inside to Joanie," Dev said. "Have her fill it with warm water."

While he waited for Jimmy Joe, he gave Kyle a call. The officer reported that all was quiet at the Winchester mansion. When Jimmy reappeared, Dev sat him down on a bench. "You've got a choice here, James. You owe Feller for those tires and whatever else you took home that night. Now, if you aren't interested in restitution, I can run you in right now and you'll have the very first entry on your juvenile record at age sixteen. But if you want to take a different path, I can help you. What's it going to be?"

The boy thought about the question for a long time, much longer than necessary as far as Dev was concerned. "I—I guess I want to do the right thing."

"Jobs are hard to come by in this town, so you are now our newest entrepreneur."

"Yeah?"

"You have a window-washing business." As he described the steps to washing the huge plate-glass windows of the café, Dev pulled out the scrub brush and then the squeegee, demonstrating how to get the glass to shine in the sunlight.

Dev stood back and watched as Jimmy Joe took care of the other side. The boy quickly corrected his mistakes, and after another squeegee the glass was streak free.

"Done," Jimmy Joe said.

"Not yet. Now you go inside and you tell Joanie to come out here and look at her window. If she likes the job, ask if she'd pay you for the job."

"How much?"

"What do you think it's worth?"

Dev could see the wheels turning in the kid's head. He stared down the street. "I could wash all these windows. Even the buildings that are closed. It would make them look much better. Ten dollars."

"Why don't you do the first job for five and if she asks you back, you'll charge her ten a week."

"Every week? That's forty dollars a month."

"The car dealership has a lot more windows. You could charge them twenty."

Dev left Jimmy Joe in front of Zelda's, adding up his potential profits as he gathered up his new equipment. If Dev was right about the kid, his investment in equipment would pay off in the end. "One at a time," he murmured to himself as he headed over to the Winchester place.

As he drove onto Wisteria Street, Dev noticed the cluster of cars parked in front of the mansion. Cursing beneath his breath, he hit the lights and the siren and raced up the street, coming to a stop in front of the mansion.

A crowd of men was gathered outside the front gate. Thankfully, someone in the group understood the meaning of "trespassing." They were shouting at the house, and he saw Elodie and his mother standing on the porch, watching the scene unfold nervously.

He found Kyle in the midst of the small gathering, arguing with a slightly inebriated Jeb Baylor. Dev stepped though the group and nodded at his junior officer. "I told you to call me if there was trouble."

"I thought I could handle it. They've had a few beers and are just letting off a little steam."

"All right," Dev said. "Everyone just settle down. Who here is carrying a gun?" Two of the men raised their hands.

"We have permits," one of the men said.

"That's fine. Kyle, take the two of them over to the car and check those permits for me. As for the rest of you, I know you're upset and these wounds run real deep. But Elodie Winchester can't help you."

"She and her family walked away with all the cash. They owe us something."

"You got something. You settled your pension case in court three years ago. It's over."

"It's not over," Jeb said. "We want answers."

"Well, Jeb, why don't you write down your questions and I'll see if Miss Elodie would be interested in answering them in a more civilized setting. Take the boys here and sit down. Put everything on paper and

I'll talk to her. She says she's going to be here for at least a week."

That seemed to pacify the crowd and they gradually dispersed. Kyle walked over, an apologetic look on his face. "Sorry, boss."

"Two of those guys had guns and they were all drinking. It could have gone bad real quick. Your first duty was to call for backup."

"It won't happen again," he said.

"No, it won't. Now I'm going to ask you to take my mother home. Stop by the grocery store if she needs to pick up something for dinner."

Dev grabbed his own grocery bags from the back of the cruiser, then strode up the front walk.

"Thank goodness you're here," his mother said. "Those men were very angry."

"Mom, Kyle is going to take you home."

"But I have more work to do," she said.

"No," Elodie said. "You've been wonderful, but Dev is right. It's time to go home."

"I'll be back tomorrow," Mary said.

Elodie glanced over at Dev, and he gave her a shrug. "Come at ten," she said. "No earlier."

"Good," Mary said. "That will give me a chance to shop for supplies."

She ran inside to collect her things, then hurried down the walk to Kyle's squad car. Dev turned to Elodie and held up the shopping bags. "I picked up a few groceries for you. I wasn't sure whether you wanted to be seen around town."

"I guess everyone knows I'm here. What was that all about? What did those men want?"

"Why don't we go around to the back? There's a nice breeze from that direction."

He followed her along the veranda, and when they reached the rear of the house, Dev set the bags down and pulled out a bottle of white wine. It was still cold. He grabbed the package of plastic cups and handed them to her.

"You bought me wine?"

"I figured you might need a few necessities. I also got you coffee, some bread and eggs. Ham. You drink wine, right?"

"I drink wine all the time," she said. She tore open the package of cups and handed him two. "And it is nearly four, so I think we're safe. My mother always said a proper lady never has alcohol before four p.m. Except at weddings and funerals."

"I'm the last guy who wants to break the rules," Dev said.

They sat down on the porch steps, staring out onto what was left of the gardens. Everything was overgrown and had long ago gone to seed. A few rosebushes still bloomed, but most of the rest was brown and dry from the heat. Dev glanced over at Elodie and caught her staring at him. He smiled. God, she was beautiful, and not in that overblown, beauty-queen style that so many women favored.

She had the elegance of another time, a past when women weren't judged based on their surgically enhanced breasts and carefully applied cosmetics. She had a simple, natural beauty that came from a lucky combination of genes and attitude. Elodie had never been conscious of how sexy she really was, and that's exactly why he'd fallen in love with her all those years ago.

"Are you going to tell me what that was all about?" she asked.

"You need to be careful around town. There are still a lot of hard feelings, especially over what your family did with the millworkers' pension money."

"I can understand that. It was a terrible thing my father did, to steal their security. He should have realized long before that time that he was in trouble. And if I could give that money back to them, I would. There's just nothing left."

"They don't know that. They assume that your family took it all and got out of town."

"That's not true," Elodie said. "We had what was left in the trust funds that our grandfather gave us, but that couldn't be touched in the lawsuit. I gave most of my trust money to my mother. She was devastated by all of this."

"How is she?"

"After the divorce, she went to live with her sister in San Diego. She has a job that she loves and a few grandchildren. It's as if her life here in Winchester never existed. She never talks about it—or my father. I think he's still in love with her, but the betrayal was just too much for her to forgive." She leaned back against the porch post and sighed softly. "I'm glad I wasn't here at the end."

"Why is that?" Dev asked.

"My memories of this house weren't spoiled. I think about this place all the time. I loved my life here, until they sent me away."

"What happened to you?" Dev asked.

"Swiss boarding school," she said. "It was just one of those extravagant expenses that brought the family business down. And all to keep me away from you." She laughed softly. "And here I am anyway."

"Because of the house," he said.

"I wanted to see it once more," she said. "I never expected to find you here. I thought you'd get out of this town as soon as you could."

"I did, but I came home. Even then, I didn't plan to stay for long, but things just happened. And now I've got a job that I love and people who need me."

"But no wife," she said.

"Ah, I see you've been talking to my mother." A blush colored her cheeks and she covered her face. "Don't worry. I don't mind. It means I have the right to ask about you. You're not married?"

She shook her head. "No."

"Why is that?"

"I guess I've just been looking for someone…special," she said. "I almost got married, but then I realized I wasn't really doing it for the right reasons."

"What happened?"

"I was twenty and had met a man who swept me off my feet. And, in the beginning, it felt like what we had when we spent that whole summer together. It was exciting and passionate and I thought I was in love. But I was just trying to re-create a happier time."

"I guess we never had a chance to find out whether we'd last," he said.

"We were so young and so crazy," Elodie said. "I lived on those memories for years."

"Me, too." He paused. "You never wrote or called."

She reached for the wine bottle and added more to her cup. "You didn't, either."

"Your father told me that if I tried to contact you, he'd fire my mother and evict us from our house."

"He told me the same thing. I guess I figured you'd find someone else. You were too charming and handsome to be single for long."

"You give me too much credit," he teased. "Nowadays, I can barely find a date."

"I don't believe that."

"No one wants to date the police chief. It's like dating a minister. You can never really enjoy yourself."

"I'm having a good time now," she said.

"Sure, now. But if you get too drunk, I'll throw you in jail," he said.

They spent the next two hours sipping wine and reminiscing about the past, though Dev limited himself to one glass because he was still on duty.

The party came to an end when the lineman from the power company appeared to turn on the electricity.

Dev figured it was a good time to say goodbye, but he didn't want to. He wanted to spend the rest of the night with her, indulging in more wine and sharing supper, but he knew better than to get greedy. He'd see her again and maybe they'd try to recapture what they once had. But he knew better than to look beyond a week or two with Elodie Winchester. She was here only until she'd "tied up loose ends," as she'd called them, with the house and then she'd be gone again.

Sadly, Elodie was probably the last Winchester who'd set foot in Winchester. And in a week or two, she'd go back to the life she'd built for herself. There was nothing for her here except this house, and she'd already said she was willing to give it away.

And yet, what could it hurt to enjoy the short time they had together? It might ruffle some feathers, but once she was gone, he could smooth those down. Right now, he was grateful for small miracles—especially the one that had brought her back into his life.

ELODIE WOKE TO the sound of thunder. She rubbed her eyes, surprised that she'd managed to sleep at all. The empty house was filled with odd noises, rattles and thumps and snaps that were no longer familiar. And her mind had been racing all day long, from the moment she'd set eyes on Dev Cassidy.

With a groan, she sat up in bed and scrubbed her face with her hands. A breeze buffeted the lace curtains on the window, and she flopped back and enjoyed the cool wind teasing her damp skin. She'd forgotten how hot the summers were in the South, how still the air became before a thunderstorm. She'd also forgotten how sweet the smell of flowers drifting on the air could be—honeysuckle and jasmine and wisteria. And most of all, she'd forgotten how easily Dev Cassidy could occupy her mind.

By most standards, they'd had an almost chaste relationship as teenagers. Though they'd danced around the edge of what might be considered sex, they'd never given in to those urges. Elodie had been terrified of pregnancy and Dev had been terrified of her father. But now, as a fully experienced woman, Elodie couldn't help but wonder what surprises and pleasures a night in bed with Dev might yield.

Even fully dressed, it was clear that he had a beautiful body. And he'd always been kind and generous, and even as a seventeen-year-old, his kissing skills had been exemplary. He'd known how to use his tongue and his lips to great effect. She wondered if he'd become even more of an expert over the years.

Thunder rumbled again, and few seconds later a flash of lightning illuminated the room. Elodie swung her legs off the bed and pulled a light cotton dress from her bag. Tugging the fabric over her head, she walked to the window overlooking the street.

The wind rustled the towering maples that lined the curb. Her gaze came to rest on a car parked in front of the house. Elodie frowned. It was a police cruiser. Was Dev having her watched? Was he afraid those men might come back in the middle of the night? If he was, why hadn't he warned her?

Elodie hurried downstairs and threw open the front door. The first spattering of rain began to hit the porch floor. She stepped out into the storm, running across the lawn. When she reached the car, she stood in front of the police car.

"What are you doing out here?" she shouted above the wind and the storm.

Dev slowly got out of the car, his hand braced along the top of the door. "I couldn't sleep."

"I couldn't, either," she shouted.

It was all he needed. He stepped toward her and before she knew it, she was in his arms, his hands smoothing over the rain-soaked fabric of her dress. His lips covered hers in a desperate, deeply powerful kiss.

Nothing about this reminded her of the past. This passion between them was fresh and raw and filled with undeniable need. His fingers tangled in her hair and he molded her mouth to his, still searching for something even more intimate.

The fabric of her dress clung to her skin, a feeble barrier to his touch. She might as well have been naked.

Elodie fought the urge to reach for the hem of her dress and pull it over her head. They were on a public street, with houses all around. Someone might be up at this hour, watching the storm.

"Come with me," she murmured, her fingers skimming over his face. She laced her fingers through his and pulled him toward the house.

Once they reached the protection of the veranda, where it was dark and none of the neighbors would see them, he grabbed her waist again, pulling her into another kiss. Dev smoothed his hand up her torso until he found her breast and he cupped it, his thumb teasing at her taut nipple.

He was impossible to resist. She couldn't form a single rational thought, even if her life depended upon it. Every reaction to his touch and kiss, to his taste and smell, was purely instinct.

Elodie reached for the hem of his shirt, but it was tucked in his trousers and his belt was hidden by his leather utility belt. "Take this off," she murmured, frantically searching for the buckle.

She stood back and watched as he carefully unclipped his gun and set it on a nearby table. A moment later, his utility belt dropped to the ground, followed by his badge and, finally, his shirt.

Her palms skimmed over hard muscle and smooth skin. His shoulders, once slight, were now broad, his torso a perfect vee.

Dev dragged her into his arms again, cupping her face in his hands as he kissed her.

"Tell me what you want," he murmured. "I'll give you anything you ask for."

She wanted him deep inside her, moving slowly, their bodies melding into one. But she had surrendered so quickly. It hadn't even been twenty-four hours. Though she'd always been able to trust him with her heart, for Elodie, this was something more.

In the fantasies she'd imagined of them making love, it had always been perfection between them, the ultimate joining of desire and romance, of need and satisfaction. It all clicked as if they'd been made for each other all along.

But what if the fantasy was nothing like reality?

Dev reached for the hem of her dress and bunched it in his fists, pulling it higher and higher until it was twisted around her waist. He gently pushed her back against the door, and she moaned as his fingertips skimmed the soft skin of her inner thigh.

Wild sensations raced through her body and she trembled as she anticipated what would come next. When he slipped his fingers between her legs, delving into the soft heat he found there, Elodie moaned.

Every nerve in her body trembled with pleasure, and she was grateful for his arm around her waist. Her legs felt weak and her knees wobbly. The only safe place for them both was her bed, but she wasn't sure they'd be able to make it all the way upstairs without being overwhelmed by their need.

A moment later, she didn't care. As he slowly began to stroke her, she could no longer think. Her attention was solely focused on his touch, on the sensations his fingers created as he brought her closer and closer to the edge.

His touch took her higher and higher, until her whole body trembled in anticipation.

When her release finally came, it stole her breath away, her body twisting and shuddering beneath his hand. She gasped with each spasm, caught up in the pleasure and barely aware of her surroundings. The intensity was almost more than she could bear, and she finally pressed her hand against his chest. "Stop," she pleaded. "I'm going to fall over."

"I have you," he said. "I won't let go."

She sank against him, and he scooped her up into his arms and opened the door, carrying her toward the stairs. But then his radio split the silence. "Winchester zero-one, this is county dispatch. Winchester zero-one, this is dispatch, come in."

Dev cursed beneath his breath. "Can you stand, Elodie?"

Elodie nodded and he placed her back on her feet. She watched as he retrieved his radio from where he'd left his utility belt. "This is Winchester zero-one. Go ahead, dispatch."

"We have a 10-50 on River Road one half mile north of the Quentin Gap Bridge. Paramedics en route. Please provide backup for Yancey County six-nine."

"I'm on my way, dispatch. Winchester zero-one, over."

Dev picked up his shirt and tugged it over his head. "I have to go," he said.

"What is it?"

"A traffic accident. About seven miles out of town."

"Is it serious?"

"I'm not sure. I'll find out when I get there. Will you be all right?"

Elodie nodded. "I—I'm fine. Will you come back?"

"If I can, I will." He fastened his utility belt around his waist, then clipped his gun holster to it. In just a few long strides, he crossed the entry hall and pulled her into his arms. His lips came down on hers and he left her with a soul-shattering kiss.

"How the hell am I supposed to concentrate on work now?"

"Try?" she said.

He chuckled softly, then stole one last kiss before heading out the door. Elodie slowly lowered herself to sit on the bottom stair, plucking at her damp dress until it hung loosely around her legs.

Never in her wildest dreams had she thought the day would turn out this way. But now that it had, Elodie had to wonder whether there was anything that would entice her to leave Winchester again.

THE SUN WAS already well over the eastern horizon when Dev and the boys from the county sheriff's office finished up the investigation of the accident. They'd found open containers in each car and had determined that both drivers had been at the same party and had challenged each other to a road race.

Unfortunately, both of the boys had ended up racing to the trauma center in Asheville in a Flight-for-Life helicopter. Though they'd both been conscious when found, Dev knew that didn't always mean a good outcome.

His handheld squawked, and he glanced at his watch then waited for Sally's voice. "Winchester zero-one, this is dispatch."

"Mornin', Sally," he said.

"Mornin', boss. I just had a call from Elodie Winchester. She said someone just threw a brick through her front window. Do you want to take this or should I send Kyle?"

Dev cursed beneath his breath. "I've got it." Though he'd spent most of the early-morning hours focused on the accident investigation, there had been moments when his thoughts had shifted back to what had happened in the mansion on Wisteria Street.

The attraction between them was undeniable, but the fact that they'd chosen to act on it so quickly was what had rattled him. It had been over ten years since they'd last seen each other, and yet it seemed as if barely a week had passed. All the old feelings were still there, the crazy, urgent need and the sense that they were hurtling toward something neither one of them could handle.

And yet, they were adults now and fully responsible for their actions. He'd given her every chance to refuse his advances and she'd just invited him to take more. Nothing had changed. Yet, everything had changed. He was responsible for her safety; he'd gone to the house to protect her, not seduce her on the porch of her house.

Dev pulled the cruiser out onto the highway and flipped on the lights and sirens. He had suspected that the anger toward Elodie wouldn't subside. He should have put another cruiser in front of her house. People in town had suffered deep wounds because of the Winchester family and they finally had someone—a flesh-and-blood person—to blame.

But it wasn't just blame. They wanted retribution, to make sure the Winchesters experienced pain as they'd experienced pain, and Dev wasn't about to let that happen. He was as angry as any of them at old man Winchester and his sons, who had all mismanaged the mill. But Elodie hadn't even been living in the town when the worst of it had gone down. Their teenage infatuation had ensured that.

Dev turned off the siren as he rolled into town. There was no traffic to contend with on his way to Elodie's street; the townsfolk were just starting to rise for the day ahead. He skidded to a stop beneath a cool canopy of trees and jumped out of the cruiser, then hurried up the brick walk.

He found Elodie sitting in a wicker rocker on the porch, sipping at a mug of coffee. Next to her, Jeb Baylor was sprawled in the opposite chair, his chin buried in his chest, a loud snore breaking the silence with every breath he took. She smiled as Dev approached.

He took the steps two at a time and crossed to her as she stood. Gathering her into his arms, he gave her a fierce hug. "What the hell is going on here?"

"It's nothing. He was drunk and upset."

"Jeb threw the brick?"

Elodie nodded. "Yes. He was shouting and I invited him up to the porch for coffee so we could talk about his concerns. But when I got back with the coffee, he was asleep. I was afraid to wake him."

Dev pressed his lips against her forehead, the sweet scent of her hair teasing at his nose. "You're safe. That's all I care about."

"What are we going to do with him? I don't want you to put him in jail. He was drunk and I don't blame him for being angry."

"He'll have to pay for the property damage," Dev said.

Elodie nodded.

Dev pulled his radio off his belt. "Winchester dispatch, this is zero-one."

"What's up, boss?"

"Call Jenny Baylor and have her come by the Winchester mansion to get her husband."

"Got it."

Dev turned back to Elodie, gently taking the mug from her hand. He took a long sip of the barely warm brew and sighed. "Do you think I could have a cup of that? Only one that's very hot?"

"Sure," Elodie said. She started toward the door, then paused, looking over her shoulder at him. "I don't know how you like your coffee. You didn't drink coffee when you were younger."

"Black," Dev said.

"Of course. Black," she murmured.

Dev walked to the opposite end of the porch, then removed his utility belt and hung it over the rail. The porch swing beckoned, and he sat down and sighed softly. Exhaustion overwhelmed him, and he tipped his head back and closed his eyes. But sleep wasn't waiting for him.

Images of Elodie swirled in his head, her body clothed, her body naked, her hair drawn away from her face, then tumbling around her shoulders. She'd been home less than twenty-four hours and he was already obsessed.

Dev cursed softly and opened his eyes. He'd always maintained such a tight control on his romantic life. Small-town gossip mills were always looking for new fodder, and he didn't want his authority being undermined by ridiculous speculation over his sex life. And they'd have a field day if he started seeing Elodie Winchester.

Elodie reappeared a few moments later, carrying a tray with two cups of steaming coffee and a pair of scones. "It's all I could manage," she said. "I don't have much in the way of groceries, save for what you gave me yesterday, and we pretty much polished that off last night. I picked up the scones yesterday. You do like scones?"

"I don't think I've ever had one," he said. "I'm pretty much a doughnut kind of guy."

She giggled as she handed him a mug. "You look like you only eat healthy. Or is it healthily?"

"I try. But it's not much of a priority. I eat when I have a chance and usually it's whatever is convenient."

"You need a wife," she said.

He growled softly, shaking his head. "I'm not so sure. That hasn't really been a priority, either."

She sat down beside him and took a sip of her coffee. "What *is* a priority for you?"

"Keeping this town from falling apart," he said.

"It's a noble goal," she murmured.

They sat silently after that, the swing creaking beneath them as they drank their coffee.

He wanted to pull her into his arms and kiss her, to find out if the attraction they'd acted upon last night was still as powerful in the morning light. But starting any kind of relationship would be complicated at best and dangerous at worst. Perhaps it was sensible to slow down and consider the consequences of a full-on affair with Elodie. Such as what she had to go back to.

"What about you?" he asked. "You haven't told me much about your life in New York."

"I managed an art gallery. I was involved with a sculptor. Very talented, but very…difficult."

"Involved?"

"We lived together for the past three years. But five days ago I walked into our loft and found him in bed with someone other than me, so I packed my bags and came home. At least to the closest thing I still have to a home."

"Do you still love him?"

Elodie smiled. "I'm not sure I ever did," she murmured. "I'm actually happy it's over. He was very high maintenance. Selfish."

"I'm glad you decided to come home," he said.

She sighed. "I don't know what to do here. This house is just…overwhelming. There's so much to fix and I can't afford the maintenance. No one wants to buy it. I'm not sure the town will even take it if I try to give it to them."

"How would that work?"

"I'd deed it to the town or the county. I've been trying to arrange that, but neither party seems interested." She took another sip of her coffee. "I suppose I could always just set it on fire and collect the insurance."

Dev cleared his throat. "You do realize that you just admitted your intention to commit a felony to a law enforcement officer."

Elodie raised one brow and gave him a playful smile. "Are you going to arrest me? Put me in handcuffs and throw me into jail?"

"Not unless you go through with your plan," he said.

"The truth is, I don't want anything to happen to this house. I love this place. I'm just not sure I can keep it."

"There has to be something, some way for you to save it. We just have to find it."

"We?"

"I'll help you," he offered. Dev didn't want to seem too enthusiastic. Keeping her in town might be good for him, but if others like Jeb made more trouble, it would only hurt the town he loved.

She nodded, then turned her attention to her coffee again. "I don't want to take advantage of you," she said. "I've only been here a day and you've been so generous. I have to start taking care of these things on my own."

"I'm sure you're very capable," he said. "But if you need help, you can always call me."

"Well, one last favor. Can you recommend someone to fix that window?" she asked.

"Come on, let's take a look. I may have just the person."

The screech of tires on the street caught their attention, and Dev watched as Jenna Baylor strode up the front walk, her damp hair pulled into a haphazard ponytail and her feet bare. Dev took a step toward her, but she held up her hand to ward him off.

Dev wasn't quite sure what she planned to do, but he could see the anger in her eyes. Would she attack Elodie or him? But in the end, she turned to her husband, crossing the veranda to stand in front of him.

She kicked Jeb's calf, and he jerked awake, rubbing his eyes against the early morning light. "What?" he mumbled.

"Get up and get your sorry ass off this porch," she said.

"What? What are you doing here?"

"I'm here to take you home. You threw a brick

through a window. And now I'm going to have to work overtime to pay for your stupid behavior." She kicked him again. "Stand up and get in that car. You need to spend more time looking for a job and less time drinkin' away the day."

Jeb stumbled off the porch, rubbing his shin as he limped down the front walk. Jenna stopped in front of Dev. "I'm sorry about this. Of course, I'll pay for the damage."

Elodie stepped out from behind Dev. "No," she said. "It's all right. There's insurance on the house. I'll just say one of the neighborhood kids did it. With a base-ball."

Jenna took a deep breath, then nodded. "Thank you, Miss Winchester. I appreciate your generosity. And I'll make sure he doesn't turn up here again. You have my word on that."

"You can call me Elodie. And if he does show up again, I'll call you directly."

Dev waited until the Baylors had driven off before he faced Elodie. "That was nice of you," he said.

"If I'm going to live here, I better try to repair some of the damage my father did before he left."

"*Are* you going to live here?" Dev asked.

Elodie shrugged. "I don't know. Not if people keep throwing bricks through my windows."

Dev slipped his arm around her waist and pulled her into a hug. But his radio interrupted his plans to steal a kiss.

"Work calls," she said.

"I guess I better check in. But I'll see you later. I

should give you my number. Where's your phone?" She handed him her cell and he entered his number into her phone book. "Call me if you have any more problems."

She took back her phone and gave him a wave as he walked out to the street. Dev paused at the cruiser and took a long look at her. Summer in Winchester had never appeared more beautiful, he mused.

3

"HELLO? MISS WINCHESTER? Anybody home?"

The feminine voice echoed through the empty house. Elodie tugged off the rubber gloves she was wearing to scrub the tile backsplash in the kitchen and dropped them next to the sink. "Just a moment," she called. Mary was cleaning in the library, and Elodie didn't want the older woman to rush to get the door.

A few seconds later, Elodie exited the kitchen and walked the length of the front hall. A dark-haired woman stood squarely in the doorway, her features softened by the thin mesh of the screen. Elodie smoothed her damp hands over her skirt before opening the door. "Hello," she said. "Are you Susanna?"

"I am," the woman said. "Susanna Sylvestri. Dev called and said you might need my help with a window repair."

"Yes, it's over here." Elodie stepped out onto the porch and led Susanna over to the broken window. "Dev mentioned you can fix leaded glass."

"I can," she said.

Like many of the townsfolk, Susanna Sylvestri regarded Elodie with a healthy dose of suspicion. She hadn't managed to smile yet and didn't seem anxious to engage in idle chitchat. "How long have you been working with glass?"

"For ten years," she said. "At first it was a hobby. Now it supports our family." Susanna paused. "My husband worked at the mill. So did my daddy and my older brother."

A long silence grew between them, and Elodie felt her spirits sag. Was it any wonder that she was roundly hated here in town? "Well, I'm glad to find you. Vintage leaded glass is tricky to repair. Whatever it costs, I'm willing to pay."

"I don't need charity," Susanna muttered, staring up at the window. "None of us do."

Elodie watched in silence as Susanna carefully removed the leaded panel from the window frame. "I can replace this plate glass, too," she said. "Although, they'd do it for cheaper at the hardware store in Hightop, or in Asheville." She ran her gloved hand over the jagged edge of glass. "It's a shame. This is the original hand-blown glass. It's been in this window since the house was built in the 1880s."

"You know a lot about the house?"

"I know a lot about glass," she said with a reluctant smile. "We might have some problems with these bevels, though," she said. "They might be hard to find."

"Actually, there's a bin of them out in the carriage house," Elodie said. "I can show you."

Susanna nodded and the two of them walked off the porch and circled around the corner of the house. "Do you just do repairs on leaded glass or do you have a studio?"

"A studio?"

"Yes, a place where you can work and sell your art. I used to run a gallery in New York and we did very well with our glass artists."

"My studio is our old chicken coop," she said. "Nothing fancy."

They retrieved the bin of glass scraps and to Susanna's surprise, she found a match for the broken bevels in the window. The woman began to relax a bit more, and Elodie tried her best to keep the conversation light, but interesting. Susanna appeared to be about four or five years older than Elodie, but her pretty face was worn by the difficulties she'd had in her life.

Elodie couldn't help but feel a measure of guilt. So many people had suffered after her father had run the mill into the ground and then pillaged his employees' pensions. "Do you sell your work anywhere?"

"I mostly do commissions," she said. "Church windows, primarily. I can't afford to make anything that might not sell. I guess that's what separates the craftspeople from the real artists."

"Still, I'd love to see your work," Elodie said.

"I have a couple of windows in my truck," she said. "I could show you. They're for a Unitarian church over in Asheville."

"Sounds great," Elodie said.

Elodie helped her gather up her tools, and Susanna

grabbed the broken window before they headed out to the street. She drove a battered panel truck, and Elodie could read the remains of the former owner's business—an automotive supply shop that had closed years ago in downtown Winchester.

Susanna opened the back door of the truck, rolling it up until the interior was exposed. She jumped up, then offered a hand to Elodie. The temperature inside was stifling, but once Elodie saw the windows, she forgot all about the heat.

"You did the design on these?" she asked, peering at the windows through the protective crating.

"I did."

"These are lovely. Stunning. You may not think it, but you *are* an artist."

Susanna laughed softly. "No, I'm not."

"Yes, you are. You ought to start believing it. If I saw this work in New York, I'd try to get you to do a show for our gallery. I'd call a few of our patrons and convince them to sponsor you. I'd make sure you had everything you needed to do your best work."

"I—I don't understand," Susanna said. "How do you make that happen?"

"I just do. I know that your business pays the bills," she said. "But maybe it's time to make room for your art."

Susanna shrugged. "I don't know. I'm barely making ends meet as it is. I'm not sure there is any room in my life for art." She drew a deep breath, then held out her hand. "It was a pleasure meeting you, Miss Winchester."

"You can call me Elodie," she said, taking her hand.

"Elodie." Susanna paused. "You're not anything like I thought you'd be."

Elodie blinked in surprise. "What did you expect?"

"Someone…different. You know, kind of snooty. I didn't expect you to be so real. Normal. Nice."

"I hope we can be friends," Elodie said.

Susanna nodded as she locked the back door of the truck. "I'll put your window at the top of the list," she said. "And I'll be here tomorrow morning to reglaze that big one."

She waved as the truck pulled away from the curb, and Elodie smiled. For the first time since she'd returned to Winchester, she felt as though she might not be Public Enemy Number One. She'd made a friend— of sorts. And she'd also come up with an idea, a tiny kernel of a concept that was beginning to take root in her mind.

Elodie hurried back to the house and walked inside, the screen door slamming behind her. She slowly took in the interior space, the walls, the doorways, the front hall. Then she ran into the empty parlor to the right of the front door. The room was full of natural light and would make a beautiful gallery.

The dining room was even better, and she tried to imagine the different ways she could use the space. What better purpose for the old mansion than to turn it into a cultural gathering point for the town?

Some of the upstairs rooms could serve as offices or meeting rooms. The ballroom could be used for presentations or guest speakers, or as a temporary gallery for traveling shows. And there were so many local artists who could benefit from their work being shown to the public.

Elodie pressed her hand to her chest, her heart beating a bit faster with excitement for the plan. The best part of it was that she could actually save the mansion and restore her family name in Winchester.

She walked into the kitchen and grabbed her cell phone, then scrolled through her numbers until she got to Dev's. But then she stopped and thought about what she was doing. Was this really about the town or was it simply an excuse to spend more time with the sexy police chief?

Her original plan had been to spend a week or two getting the house in order and then finding a way to cut her final ties to the town. And now, all she could think about was seeing more of Dev.

A warm flush crept up her cheeks, and she sighed softly, remembering very clearly the effect his touch had on her body. That first sexual encounter had come as a complete surprise, the desire between them so intense that it had overwhelmed every last shred of her common sense—they'd almost made love on her porch, for goodness' sake.

It wasn't as if she were accustomed to seducing strangers. Elodie had enjoyed four or five serious relationships in her life, and in between, she'd dated a number of handsome, successful and eligible New York City bachelors. But not a single man outside of Dev Cassidy had ever made her behave with such reckless abandon.

Smiling, she set the phone back down on the counter, then sat down on an old kitchen stool. Maybe she ought to give this plan a few days to percolate in her brain. Right now, it appeared to be the answer to all her problems—it gave her a home, a job, a place to belong. But all of that was twisted up around the man.

"Miss Elodie?"

She glanced up to find Mary Cassidy standing in the doorway. "Oh, Mary, I'd almost forgotten you were here. You should have gone home ages ago."

"I wanted to finish oiling the paneling in the library. I came across something you might want to see."

Elodie followed Mary through the house. When they got to the library, the scent of beeswax and lemon permeated the air. It was a smell she remembered well from her childhood, and she smiled. "This looks lovely," she said, taking in the soft sheen on the cherry paneling.

"Thank you, but this is why I brought you in here," Mary said, pointing to a small panel beneath one of the bookcases. "I was rubbing the wax into the wood and it just popped open. It's a secret storage spot."

Elodie frowned. "Is there anything in there?"

"I didn't look. It wasn't my place."

Elodie bent down and peeked into the dark recesses of the library wall. "It seems empty," she said. She closed the door, noting the location of the latch, then gave the panel a good push. It popped open again. "Interesting. Too bad there aren't any family jewels that my ancestors hid away. They'd help pay for a new roof."

"There are a lot of files left in your father's desk, though," Mary said. "You should probably go through those and see if there's anything important."

"I will," Elodie said. She sat down in the battered leather chair behind the desk, then slowly turned it in a complete circle. "Just another thing to add to my list."

"Maybe I should start coming an hour earlier," Mary said.

"No," Elodie replied. "Mary, I can't afford to pay you for the time you're already putting in."

"You don't have to—"

"Yes, I do. A few hours a day is fine. But you've been spending your entire day here."

"When you sell the house, you can pay me," Mary said. "Or not. I just want to help out."

Elodie pushed out of the chair and crossed the room to Mary. She looped her arm though the older woman's, then drew her along to the door. "Why don't we take a break and have some sweet tea and a few of those cookies you brought me."

As they walked back through the house, Elodie made a mental note to talk to Dev about his mother's determination to resume her old duties. As much as her help was appreciated, Elodie was in no position to pay her. Maybe Dev could convince her to stay home.

She wondered if she ought to call him. He'd called her last night and again early this morning, but he hadn't suggested they get together. Perhaps he regretted what had happened that first night. If people in town found out they were involved in a sexual relationship, it could mean trouble—for both of them.

If he'd decided to stay away, she had to trust that Dev knew what was best. But that didn't mean she had to like it.

IT WAS DEV'S favorite time of day, when most of the citizens of Winchester were through with their supper and settling in for the evening, maybe watching a ball game, maybe relaxing on the porch as they searched for a cool breeze or the scent of rain.

His shift was over at 10:00 p.m., and as he got closer to that time, his mind was increasingly occupied with thoughts of Elodie. He'd made a point to stay away from the mansion on Wisteria Street at night, knowing that the temptations there were just too great to deny. But he had checked in with her, and she seemed to be busy working on the house.

He had the day off tomorrow and had decided to find a way to spend it with Elodie. He could help with some of the work around the house, maybe do some painting or clean up the brush in the old gardens.

Just the thought of returning to her orbit made him a bit uneasy. It took all his strength to keep from touching her, and his mind was constantly filled with seductive images of their intimate encounter on her porch. It seemed like a dream, he mused. As if he'd somehow imagined it. Would it happen again? Could he make it happen again? Should he?

He kept telling himself that caution was the key, and he hoped going over there during the day would keep him from kissing her and hauling her off to the bedroom. There were more excuses during daylight hours.

Dev glanced at the clock on the dash, then pulled the cruiser over to the curb in front of Zelda's. A cup of coffee should give him enough energy to finish off his shift. But he knew he was in for another restless night.

He hadn't slept well since Elodie had arrived in town, and he didn't expect that would change anytime soon.

The café was almost empty when he stepped inside. He slid onto a stool at the counter, then fixed his eyes on the refrigerated case next to the cash register. A few seconds later, Joanie walked up, the coffeepot in her hand. She flipped a cup over in a saucer and poured.

"Quiet night?" she asked.

"Yeah. I'll take a slice of that cherry pie, please."

"Ice cream?"

"Sure, why not," Dev said.

She set the pie in front of him, then leaned against the counter. "Jimmy Joe's got himself quite a little enterprise, thanks to you. You just seem to watch out for everyone in this town, don't you?"

Dev looked up from his pie, the fork halfway to his mouth. "I do my job."

"People are talking," she said.

"They have a tendency to do that when they don't have better things to occupy their mind."

"Is it true that you and Elodie Winchester had a thing for each other back in the day? I've heard you're the reason she was sent away. That she got pregnant and her daddy couldn't stand the thought of the housekeeper's son and his daughter together."

Dev chuckled. "That's what they're saying? That's quite a story."

"Is it true?"

"There was no baby," Dev said.

"How do you know?"

"Because I know how babies are made and there

wasn't any of that going on between us. As for the rest of it, I guess that's close to the real story."

"And what about now?" Joanie asked. "You don't have to tell me, but I could be useful in tamping down any rumors."

"She's a beautiful woman. I find her...intriguing. Interesting. That's all."

"She's sitting over there," Joannie said. "Maybe you ought to go say hello."

Dev glanced over his shoulder. A slender figure sat with her back to him. He wouldn't have thought it was Elodie. "When did she come in?"

"She had dinner. She's using the Wi-Fi. I guess she doesn't have internet access at home." Joannie chuckled. "Nothing going on between you, huh? You look as if you've been hit by a truck."

"Keep that to yourself, would you?"

Joannie nodded, then pushed away from the counter and headed back to the kitchen. Dev picked up his coffee and pie and wandered over to Elodie's booth.

"Can I join you?"

She glanced up and met his gaze, then smiled. "Hi. Sure. Sit down."

"I didn't expect to find you here," Dev said.

"Internet access," she said. "I'm working on a—a project."

"That sounds interesting. Do you want to tell me about it?"

Elodie shook her head. "Not yet." She closed her computer and set it aside. "Are you done with work?"

"Not yet. I'm on duty until ten. Two more hours. But I have tomorrow off, so that's a good thing."

"It is," she said.

"Maybe, if you need a hand with some of your projects, I can help you out. Mom says you've been painting."

"I have. But there's so much else that has to be done. I'd be thrilled if you wanted to help."

"Great. I'll bring breakfast and we'll get an early start."

He reached for his coffee, but his radio squawked. Dev cursed softly. It seemed to be the way it went when he was with her—always interrupted by work. "Sorry," he murmured.

Dev switched on the radio and listened to the call. Kids had been spotted parked up on Spencer's Landing, a popular spot for romance, and there was suspicion of alcohol on the scene. Dev knew that the moment he pulled up, they'd scatter, but he also knew that teens driving drunk was a prescription for disaster, and if he split them up before anything got out of hand, he could save them all some trouble.

"I have to go," he said, gobbling down the rest of his pie. "I'll see you tomorrow morning."

Elodie nodded. "All right."

Dev headed for the door, then stopped and returned to her table. "Would you like to come along? After I check this out, I could drop you at your place. Unless you drove down here."

"I didn't. I walked. Sure, I can come. Where are we going?"

"Spencer's Landing," he said.

They'd spent a fair amount of time at the very spot years ago, sitting on a blanket beneath the stars, exploring the limits of teenage passion. Not that he needed a reminder of the passion they shared.

Dev waited as she gathered her things, then grabbed her computer bag as they walked to the door. "Thanks, Joannie."

"Leaving already?" she called from the kitchen.

"Duty calls," Dev said.

"Thank you," Elodie said.

When they reached the car, Dev circled around and opened the passenger side door for Elodie and he helped her inside. When he slipped behind the wheel, he found her smiling at him. "What?"

"Are you sure this is all right?"

"I'm the chief. And it's not like I'm taking you into the middle of a crisis situation. We're going to bust up a bunch of horny teenagers. And if they've been drinking, we're going call their parents, who will give them a ride home."

"Sounds like fun," Elodie said.

He started the car and pulled out into the street. "This is it," Dev admitted. "It's not Manhattan. It's not even Asheville. It's just a small town with small-town problems."

"I know. But there's something great about what you do here," Elodie said. "You turned into a very good man, Dev."

He wasn't sure why her opinion mattered so much, but it did. They'd known each other for a long time and she'd been instrumental in changing the direction of his life. Before he met Elodie, he'd been drifting, uninterested in school, searching for trouble. But after their summer together, he wanted to be better. He'd tried to make himself into the kind of man Elodie would want. He'd waited for her to come back, hoping that her father would forget what had happened and bring his only daughter home. By the time Dev realized she wouldn't return, he'd managed to graduate from high school with a B average and got into a decent college. He owed her a lot and he'd never properly thanked her.

"There is something we need to talk about," Elodie said. "It's your mother. She comes to work every day, and though I appreciate her enthusiasm, I can't really afford to pay her. I've tried talking to her about it, but she's so loyal to the family, she feels it's her duty to take care of me."

"My mother needs that job," he said. Dev glanced over at her, hoping she'd understand. But there didn't seem to be any hint of understanding in Elodie's expression. "Since you've been back, she's been so happy to have a purpose in life. For most of her life, your family was her family. And when the mill shut down and your parents left, she felt abandoned." He paused. "If she insists on being paid, then I'll give you money for her salary. Just don't let her know where it came from. Could you do that?"

Elodie nodded. "Of course I can. But I don't want her working any more than four hours a day."

"I think I can convince her to cut down on her hours."

She reached out and touched his arm. "You're so

good to her. My mother always told me that you can measure a man by how he treats his mother."

"She hasn't had an easy life," he said.

Dev slowed the cruiser as they reached the narrow dirt road that led out to the landing on the river. He looked over at Elodie to find her smiling. "Remember this?"

She nodded. "My heart is beating so fast," she said, pressing her hand to her chest. "I think I'm going to die if I don't kiss you."

"I'm trying to be cool," he said. "But it doesn't work. My hands are shaking and my palms are sweating. I'm afraid you're going to notice."

"I'm wondering if this is going to be the night we can't stop," she said.

When they reached the end of the road, they came into a clearing, a spot that was usually filled with cars and kids. But tonight, the landing was deserted. Dev pulled the cruiser to a stop and switched off the ignition. "Someone must have tipped them off."

"Better for us," Elodie said. She opened the door and got out. "Come on. Let's have a look around."

Dev watched her through the windshield of the car, the headlights shining on the pale blue dress she wore. A light breeze teased at the hem, causing the fabric to cling to her slender legs.

She looked like some forest nymph, her pale hair tumbling in waves around her shoulders. He wanted to capture her in his arms, pull her body against his and kiss her. But as he stepped out of the car, Dev clenched his fists at his side, trying to slow the rapid pounding of his heart.

He felt like a high school kid again, filled with raging hormones and self-doubt. Who was this beautiful creature and why did she hold such power over him?

Elodie turned to face him, then reached down to grab the hem of her dress. "I'm going for a swim," she said. "Do you want to come with me?"

"I'm on duty," he said.

"Then you'll just have to watch."

Dev groaned inwardly. He was already hard just thinking about Elodie naked in his arms, the warm water enveloping their bodies.

He'd been a fool to bring her here. But he didn't regret it for a moment.

ELODIE STOOD AT the water's edge, staring out onto the moonlit surface of the river. She couldn't remember the last time she'd felt this…alive. The past and the present had somehow merged and she was living out some long-ago fantasy.

This place had been part of it. He'd brought her here once before, when they were teenagers. A small group of his friends had gathered for a party and she'd sneaked out of the house to meet him. When they'd first arrived, Elodie had hoped that it might be fun, meeting some of the people he considered friends. But everyone treated her as if she were an interloper—like some foreign princess who would judge them for their public school education and discount store wardrobes.

After a lot of beer and tequila, they'd all decided to

go skinny-dipping. But Elodie couldn't bring herself to join them. She already felt vulnerable, and stripping down to her underwear wasn't going to make her feel any more secure. So she'd sat on the shore and waited for Dev.

It was the first time she'd realized that there might not be a future for the two of them. They came from very different worlds, and those worlds were being dragged further and further apart.

But now, by some strange stroke of luck, their orbits had crossed again and they were in the same place at the same time. Only now, she was in control of her life—not her father or mother, and there was no fortune to come between them.

"Come on," she said, glancing over her shoulder. "Let's go in."

"You really want to take a swim?"

She faced him, tossing her dress onto the grass by her feet. "Do you remember the first time you brought me here?"

Dev nodded. "It didn't go that well, as I recall."

"I sat on the shore, right over there, while you joined your friends for a swim." She kicked off her sandals and her toes sank into the sandy soil. "Are you going to join me now?"

"I can't. I'm on duty."

"Convenient excuse," she said. Elodie had planned to stop at her underwear but then decided he needed more of a temptation.

She wasn't that scared girl anymore and she'd conquered most of her self-doubts long ago. She was a woman who knew exactly what she wanted and right now, she wanted to feel the cool river water on her hot, salty skin. Elodie dropped her bra on top of her discarded dress, then skimmed out of her panties. The warm breeze teased at her hair and she closed her eyes and enjoyed the wild sensations racing through her body.

When she was a teenager, Winchester had seemed such a harsh, stifling place, a spot where she could never truly be herself. And now, for some odd reason, it seemed like the only place on the planet where she could live her life exactly as she pleased.

She started toward the small beach. "It sure is a warm night. That water is going to feel so nice."

"I could arrest you," he called. "For indecent exposure."

She faced him, running her hands through her hair. "You'd have to come in and get me," she said. With that, Elodie turned and waded into the river. When the water reached her knees, she dived beneath the surface. After the heat of the day, the water was barely cool, but it felt wonderful on her bare skin.

Popping up, she brushed her hair from her eyes and searched the beach for him. He was still standing there, arms crossed and fully clothed. The standoff ended when they both noticed the headlights from a car through the trees. Cursing softly, she sank down until she was nearly undetectable in the dark.

When the lights emerged into the clearing, she was relieved to see that it was another police car. From what she could tell, this was a county cop, but someone Dev seemed to know quite well. Though sound carried well in the still night air, Elodie couldn't quite make out what they were saying. It appeared that Dev was relaying the story of the party that had brought him out to the river.

A few minutes later, the cop nodded, then got into his car and drove away. Elodie started for the shore. "What did he want? Is he coming back?"

"You're in trouble now," Dev said.

"What? Did he notice me?"

"This could be very serious. The county is starting to crack down on this kind of lewd behavior."

"I'm naked," she said. "I wouldn't call myself lewd."

"Down here in the South, that's enough."

When she was out of deep water, Dev approached the shore and waited, holding out his hand. The moment she placed her fingers in his palm, he swept her into his arms, picking her up off her feet and carrying her across the sand.

He set her down next to the police cruiser, then went back to fetch her dress, shoes and underwear. He held out her bra, letting it dangle from his fingertips. "Put this on."

"Are you angry?"

"No, but I'm on duty. And this is highly inappropriate. I mean, this is a tabloid scandal waiting to happen. Local Cop Caught with Naked Heiress? Sexy Swim on Taxpayer's Dime? I can see it all now."

"I just thought it would be—"

He grabbed her shoulders and met her gaze. "Do you have any idea the strength it's taking for me not to take advantage of this situation right now? I want to pull you into my arms and run my hands all over you until there's not an inch of you left untouched."

"How long until you go off duty?" she asked. "I suppose I could wait."

He chuckled softly. "Another hour."

"And what are you going to do with me until then?" Elodie asked.

"I'm going to take you home and avoid all further temptation."

He helped her dress, and Elodie could see that he was already regretting his decision. His fingertips skimmed along her naked shoulders and his palm brushed against her breast. With each innocent caress, she felt the need growing inside her.

It was time to put an end to this simmering attraction between them, time to see exactly where their desire might take them. There was no reason to wait. "Who would have thought that I'd be the one to lose my inhibitions and you'd turn into an upright citizen? Kind of a strange switch, isn't it?"

"What are you trying to say?" Dev asked.

"I remember when you weren't afraid of anything."

"I'm not afraid," he said, his jaw tight. "I just have a lot more to lose. I was just some punk kid back then, Elodie. I didn't care about anything or anyone—except you. But I'm trying my damnedest to keep this town from crumbling into dust. Since the mill closed, a third of the population has left. Half of Main Street is boarded up. And I'm just trying to keep things in order until something or someone comes along with a lifeline."

"What kind of lifeline?"

"I don't know. Some kind of project that will bring businesses back. Some way to make this town attractive to tourists and then families."

Elodie thought again of her idea for the mansion. Could that be a starting point? The mill was standing empty. Maybe there was something to be done with that building, too? But putting Winchester back on the map was a long-term commitment. She'd come to town to take care of her own business and then leave. The last thing she wanted to do was get involved in some complicated project that might never succeed.

"You're a good man, Dev." She finished buttoning the front of her dress and then ran her fingers through her damp hair. "This town is lucky to have you."

"You make me sound like some kind of Dudley Do-Right. I'm a small-town cop," he said. "Nothing more."

She pressed her palm to his chest. "I wasn't talking about your job. I was talking about your heart. A lot of people would have walked away from this town. A lot of people did, but you chose to stay and make a difference. That's not duty. That's love."

He wrapped his arms around her and pulled her into a fierce hug. "Thank you," he murmured, pressing a kiss to her forehead.

It was amazing how they understood each other. It was as if she could read his mind, anticipate what he was going to think or say. There was something exciting in finding that kind of relationship with a man. It made him even more attractive.

He held her for a long time, the warm night breeze drying the last bit of dampness from her skin. And then, tipping her head back with the soft touch of his hand, Dev kissed her. His tongue teased at her lips, then invaded the warmth of her mouth, at first playful and then deeply passionate. There was a way he had of completely possessing her, demanding surrender no matter how innocent the encounter.

Elodie had always maintained a safe distance with the men in her life, controlling her emotions and never allowing herself to become too dependent on anyone. But with Dev, the choice was out of her hands. She trusted him. She'd known him for most of her life. And nothing she saw in the grown-up man had changed her opinion. He was still her white knight, only now he wore a badge and carried a gun.

When he finally drew away, Elodie sighed softly. It was so easy to kiss him, yet she knew with each kiss, with each intimate encounter, her choices would only grow more complicated.

4

DEV DROPPED ELODIE off with a kiss and a promise to come back when his shift was over. In turn, she promised to leave the kitchen door open.

He'd promised himself he'd stay away from her until tomorrow, but after seeing her naked, after touching her and holding her, there was no way he could wait to be with her again. But it seemed that the fates had decided to ruin yet another evening for them.

"You were caught with a gun in the car," Dev said, fixing his gaze on Jimmy Joe Babcock, who sat across from him in the interrogation room in the police station. "An unregistered gun. Do you have any idea how much trouble you're in?"

"It's not my gun," Jimmy Joe said. "I didn't even know it was in the car. I swear, I didn't."

"Whose gun is it?" Dev asked.

Jimmy Joe stared down at his hands, shifting nervously as Dev waited for an answer. "I'm not sure."

"I don't believe you."

"I can't… I can't say whose it is."

"Then you want to take the heat for something you didn't do? Jimmy, I know you want to make something of yourself."

"I do. I want to be a cop. Like you."

Dev sat back, surprised by the determination on Jimmy's young face. "You can't be a cop if you're charged with a felony. And possessing an unregistered gun is a felony." He decided not to tell Jimmy the whole truth, that he probably would be charged as a juvenile and he could probably make a deal to avoid a felony charge. But right now, Dev had some leverage and he wanted to get to the bottom of Jimmy's problems.

"Let's just say I know who this gun belongs to," Dev said. "You don't need to tell me."

Jimmy nodded. "Do you?"

"I have a few ideas. But if I bring those people in and they lay this on you, there's not much I can do. Are they going to admit the truth?"

Jimmy thought about his answer for a long moment, his lip caught between his teeth. Dev was surprised when tears began to fill his eyes. With a soft curse, he brushed them away. He slowly shook his head. "I doubt it. I think he's maybe not gonna want to go back to jail."

Both Jimmy's father and his older brother had done time, and his brother, Ray, was on parole. Until recently, it had seemed as though Jimmy was going to follow in their footsteps. But Dev had hoped that his new job might put him on the straight and narrow.

"I believe you, Jimmy."

"You do?" A look of utter relief washed over his features.

"I do. But you're going to have to make a choice. This is one of those moments when you decide the kind of man you're going to be. Are you going to stand up for what's right and true? Or are you going to make excuses for people who don't deserve your loyalty?"

Jimmy's hopeful expression faded. "Shouldn't a man try to protect his family?"

Dev pushed his chair back and stood. "Well, I guess since you're going to have to get used to living in a cell, you might as well start now. I can't do anything for you here. The county sheriff picked you up. This is their case, not mine." Dev reached in his pocket and handed Jimmy his card. "If you change your mind, you just shout and ask them to call me."

Dev walked out of the room, glancing at the clock in the hallway. It was nearly midnight and he'd promised Elodie that he'd be over two hours ago. He'd sent her a text to let her know that he'd been delayed, but she hadn't answered. At some point it was natural for her to get irritated with the demands of his job, especially considering her upbringing. But there was nothing he could do about it.

Deputy Sam Rivers walked down the hall toward Dev, Jimmy's case file in his hand. "Did he tell you anything?"

Dev sighed. "It's not his gun. I'd bet my paycheck it belongs to Ray Don, his older brother. But he won't admit to it because his brother's on probation and a gun charge will send him right back to prison. Jimmy's got to decide for himself. Let him spend the night here, but hang on to his paperwork. I'll go at him tomorrow morning again. Call his father and let him know that he's going to be charged. You're going to want to talk to Ray Don. If you can't find him, call his probation officer. If you still can't find him, let me know. I'll grab him up for you."

If Elodie weren't waiting, he'd go out and find Ray Don right that minute and haul him in before he figured out that they'd found the gun in Jimmy's car. But a hungover Ray Don was much easier to question than a belligerent drunk. Dev would sit him down in the morning and play on his brotherly love, give him a chance to do the right thing, to give Jimmy the opportunity that he never had.

Dev cursed beneath his breath. Now that he'd taken an interest in Jimmy, he couldn't just desert him, no matter who Dev had waiting for him. "Never mind. I'll call Ray Don's probation officer and find out what he's been up to. I'm going over to the house right now to talk to Jimmy's father."

In the end, he spent another two hours trying to get Jimmy out of jail and realizing that the kid had it a lot harder than Dev had ever realized. Neither his brother nor his father had any intention of copping to the gun charge, and they seemed almost relieved that Jimmy was willing to take the heat for something he hadn't done.

By 2:00 a.m., Dev wondered if he ought to just go back to his place and try to explain everything to Elodie in the morning. But he didn't want to be alone. He wouldn't be able to sleep, so why not take a chance with Elodie? Just one kiss would be enough to wipe away the frustrations of the evening.

Dev decided to leave the cruiser at his place, in case he did spend the night with her. He stripped off his uniform and shrugged into a T-shirt and a well-worn pair of cargo shorts, then put on his trainers and jogged back out into the humid night.

He started at a slow jog, breathing deeply as he listened to his footsteps on the silent street. He loved being out in the dead of night, when the town was sound asleep. Whenever he felt restless, he'd jog along the streets, enjoying the calm that always seemed to dissipate once the sun rose.

By the time he reached Elodie's neighborhood, a soft rain had begun to fall, the drops a relief on his warm skin. A distant roll of thunder brought a fresh, cool breeze, and he breathed deeply and increased his pace.

The mansion on Wisteria Street was dark as he approached. He wiped the rain from his eyes, then carefully scanned the street, wondering if there was anyone awake and watching. Then, Dev jumped over the gate and dodged through the shadows to the front door.

When he found it locked, Dev circled the house and went to the back, remembering that she'd said she'd leave the kitchen door open. But it was locked, as well. Cursing softly, he continued around the house until he stood beneath her bedroom window. The curtains fluttered against the screen and he smiled to himself.

How many times had he climbed the trellis onto the roof of the veranda and sneaked into her room late at night? She'd leave a light on, covered with a silk scarf, and be curled up in her bed, waiting. Dev closed his eyes and let the memories wash over him.

He'd always made the climb with a healthy dose of fear in his heart, praying that he wouldn't get caught by her father or one of her brothers. Now the fear came from praying he wouldn't slip and break a leg. He wasn't quite as nimble as he had been as a seventeen-year-old.

"This will make for another amusing scandal," he muttered. "Police Chief Breaks Leg Sneaking into Local Woman's Bedroom." It seemed as if every encounter with Elodie lately came with an accompanying headline.

He took a deep breath, then shimmied up the old trellis at the end of the veranda. He heard the wood snap beneath his feet, and for a moment he was afraid the whole trellis was about to come down. But it held long enough for him to grab the edge of the roof and swing himself up.

Carefully, he made his way to her window, the roof slippery beneath his feet. A small expandable screen held the window sash up, and he pulled it out. But the moment he did, the window slid down. Dev stuck his hand underneath it to keep it from slamming shut. He bit back a howl as his fingers were pinched between the frame and the sash.

By the time he pulled the sash up again, his entire hand was throbbing. He crawled through the window, then replaced the screen. Cursing softly, he rubbed his fingers until the ache subsided.

He turned and faced the bed, taking in the sight of

her, her long limbs bare, her hair spread across the pillow, her features soft and relaxed.

She wore a thin cotton nightgown that was twisted high on her thighs. Dev stood next to the bed for several minutes, just watching her sleep, listening to the even cadence of her breathing. She was the most beautiful creature he'd ever set eyes on. He'd known it that night at the Christmas party and he knew it now. There would never be another woman for Dev.

Thunder rumbled, this time louder, and he held his breath as she stirred. The last thing he wanted to do was frighten her. He tugged off his T-shirt and kicked out of his shoes, then skimmed his shorts over his hips. Holding his breath, Dev carefully sank down onto the bed, then stretched out beside her. "It's just me, Ellie," he whispered.

"What time is it?"

"It's really late."

She smiled and a long sigh slipped from her lips. He closed his eyes and allowed his body to relax. Outside, the storm intensified as lightning split the night sky and the wind rustled the trees outside the window. Though he wanted to wake her, to pull her body beneath his and make love to her, Dev was content to merely lie beside her.

She rolled over in her sleep and faced him, and Dev took her hand and pressed it against his chest. Her eyes fluttered open, and Elodie smiled again. "Did you crawl up that trellis?"

Dev chuckled. "Yes. You locked the doors."

"I got spooked. I didn't think you were coming."

"I got held up at work," he murmured. He wrapped his arm around her waist and pulled her closer. "But I'm here now."

She smiled, her eyes sleepy. "You're here." She gently pushed him back into the pillows, then crawled on top of him, her legs straddling his hips. "Now, what am I going to do with you?"

ELODIE HAD FANTASIZED about this moment so many times over the past decade. Now that he was here, lying nearly naked in her arms, any doubts she had were quickly melting away.

Though sex had always come with insecurities and regrets, Elodie refused to let that happen with Dev. For as long as they were together, she was going to enjoy him. It wasn't often a woman got a chance to relive her past, to recapture a moment that had slipped away. This was that chance, and she wanted him more than she'd ever wanted anything in her life.

She smoothed her hands over his chest, taking in the hard ripple of muscle beneath the warm skin. He had become an extraordinary man, she mused. Strong and chiseled, so different from the boy she'd known. And yet, there was still some of that boy left inside him, in the devilish glint in his eyes and the crooked smile he gave her now.

"It's strange, being in this bed and not having to worry about getting caught," Elodie said. "It's kind of liberating, isn't it?"

"We don't have to be quiet," he said. He arched beneath her, and she felt his erection between them. "We can move."

"So what should we do first? How did you imagine this might happen all those years ago?"

"I always imagined we'd both be naked," he said.

Elodie laughed. "We were both a bit shy about that. I don't think I ever saw you completely naked, not with the lights on."

He reached for the hem of her nightgown. "And I never saw you, either."

Elodie hopped off him and stood beside the bed. "I want you to see me now."

Dev rolled off the bed and stood in front of her. "Me, too."

"We'll go together," she said.

She pulled her nightgown over her head and he tossed aside his boxer shorts. They stood and stared at each other for a long moment before Elodie laughed.

"Not exactly the reaction I was hoping for," he murmured.

"No, I'm not laughing at you. You're...perfect. You're a Greek god in human form. And I'm so nervous I might pass out."

"Dressed or undressed, you're the most beautiful woman I've ever known," Dev said.

The compliment bolstered her confidence, and Elodie reached out and placed her hand on his chest. Slowly, she let her fingertips trace a path down and across his belly to his shaft, now hard and erect. She'd never really looked at him or touched him in all those months of teenage intimacies. Now, she couldn't seem to stop herself.

As she slowly began to stroke him, Dev groaned, and he reached out, furrowing his fingers through the hair at her nape. Elodie gazed up at him and found his eyes closed, intent on maintaining control. She realized then that she had a choice. This first time could be fast and fiery. Or she could make it a long, deliberate seduction. He was obviously willing to let her take the lead for now.

Elodie pressed her palm to his chest, gently pushing him back to the bed, and they tumbled down into the tangle of bed linens. His chest gleamed in the soft light from the lamp, and every now and then a flash of lightning would cast everything in a harsh gray tone.

She bent over him and traced a path of kisses across his chest, moving from one nipple to the other. He pushed up on his elbows and watched her through passion-glazed eyes, his fingers smoothing the hair away from her face. As she moved lower, following the path her hand had taken earlier, he flopped down on the bed, clutching the sheets in his fists.

The instant her tongue touched his shaft, his body jerked. And when she took him into her mouth, he moaned as if the pleasure was more like pain. But Elodie had learned a lot in the days since she and Dev had been together, and she was anxious to prove that she wasn't the same girl he'd once loved.

She was a woman, with a particular set of skills that could ensure Dev a night of intense pleasure. Using her lips and her tongue, she teased and caressed him, bringing him close to the edge before letting him slip away. Dev understood what she was doing, and he whispered desperate encouragement and then soft commands to slow down or stop. His fingers, still tangled in her hair, gently drew her away when it became too much.

Elodie knew he was dancing dangerously close to the edge, and she expected him to finally surrender, his body's need for satisfaction outweighing his ego's need for control. She drew him into her mouth again, but when she pulled back, Dev reached down and grabbed her around the waist, pulling her body along the length of his.

She wriggled around on top of him, and he held her hips tight against hers. "Don't move," he murmured.

"Why not?" she asked, shifting above him. The tip of his shaft slid along the damp crease between her legs.

"I want to get a condom."

"I've got that covered," she said. She pushed up on her knees and the next time she moved, he was there, ready to slip inside her. With a sigh, Elodie sank down on top of him.

It was the most marvelous, electrifying sensation in the world, having him, warm and hard, buried deep inside her. They'd enjoyed an emotional connection all those years ago, but this was much more than just sweet words and soft caresses. He was exposed and vulnerable, and she had his release at her command. Elodie felt powerful, yet blissfully happy at the same time.

She began to move above him, slowly at first, her palms pressed against his chest, her tongue teasing at his as they kissed. Her body reacted to each thrust with a wild rush of sensation, a current that set each nerve on fire until she could focus only on her own need.

And when he reached between them and touched her, his thumb gently massaging, Elodie realized how close to the edge she was. Instinct drove her ahead as she reached for the final wave of pleasure that would wash her into oblivion. Again and again, it was almost within her grasp, only for him to draw her away. And then, the first spasm hit and her breath caught in her throat before she dissolved into a maelstrom of pleasure.

When she was nearly finished, Dev finally let go and gave in to a powerful orgasm that left him shuddering and trembling with each movement.

Slowly, they drifted back to reality, their bodies damp with perspiration, the sheets tangled about them.

He buried his face in the curve of her neck and groaned, taking care not to move, still hard inside her. "I have to say, that was worth the wait."

Elodie laughed, and he groaned again. "Sorry," she murmured.

"I just want to stay like this for a moment. Then we'll do it all over again."

"Again?"

"I'm making up for twelve years," he said. "That's how long I've been imagining this."

She rolled to his side, draping her arm around his waist and snuggling up against him. "Is that true? Have you thought about us?"

"Sure," he said.

"What did you think about? Was it just about the sex?"

"Only sometimes. You'd appear in one of my fantasies. You know. Self-gratification."

"Really?" she said. "You do that often?"

He shrugged. "There have been some long periods where I haven't had a woman in my life and…well, a guy needs some relief."

"And when you weren't thinking about me sexually? What about then?"

He pressed his lips to her shoulder and considered her question for a long moment. "I would try to imagine you in different places, doing different things. There were nights when I'd just sit and stare at the moon, and wonder where you were and how long it might take for me to find you."

"You could have searched for me on the internet," she said. "Or found me on social media."

"I suppose I could have. But then I would have known for sure, and I would have felt compelled to do something about it. And I was pretty certain that your life out there, beyond Winchester, was better than what you would have had here with me."

"Why would you think that?" Elodie asked.

"Because you never came back," Dev said.

Elodie looked up and met his gaze. Though he was smiling, she could see tiny shards of pain in his blue eyes, memories that just wouldn't go away. She'd had the whole wide world to help her forget him. He'd had only this place, this town and the people in it.

"I'm here now," she said. "And it's not too late."

Elodie wasn't sure what she meant by those words.

Too late for what? But any regret she had in saying them was brushed aside as Dev pulled her into a long, delicious kiss.

DEV WOKE UP SLOWLY, becoming aware of his surroundings bit by bit—the feel of unfamiliar sheets beneath his naked body, the floral scent that seemed to suffuse his pillow, and the sound of trees rustling in the morning breeze.

He smiled to himself as he reached out for Elodie, the memories of the night before flooding into his mind in a rush of wild images and powerful feelings.

When he found her side of the bed empty, Dev sat up and rubbed his eyes. "Ellie?" he called.

A moment later, she appeared in the bedroom doorway, wearing his T-shirt, a tray in her hands. "Breakfast," she said with a grin. "I'm starving. What about you?"

"I could eat," he murmured.

She set the tray on the bed, then crawled in beside him. "It's nothing fancy. French toast, some fruit and coffee."

"Coffee," he said. She picked up an odd-looking glass pot and began to pour. "What's that?"

"What? The coffee? I think it's Italian roast."

"No, the pot. It looks like a beer mug."

"It's a French press," she said. "It makes really great coffee." She frowned. "You've never seen a French press before?"

"Here in Winchester," he said with a thick drawl, "all our coffee comes direct from a Mr. Coffee machine." He took a sip of the coffee and was surprised at the taste, rich and syrupy, like nuts and chocolate.

"We need to get you out into the world a little bit more," she said.

"They might have a few of these French things over in Asheville. There've been some rumors, but I'm not sure if they're true or not."

"Do you like to travel?" she asked.

"Yeah, but I haven't done much. It's not a lot of fun to go alone. Where's the joy in seeing something amazing if you don't have someone to share it with?"

"Where would you go if you could?"

"New York. LA. Australia. Spain. Egypt." He glanced at her over the rim of his cup. "I suppose you've been to all those places."

She nodded. "I have. But they're all places I'd go again. And there are lots of places that I've never been that I'd love to see."

"Well, when I inherit my millions, we'll just hop on a plane and check out the rest of the world. Although, I can't imagine any place better than Winchester." The last was laced with enough sarcasm that it brought a giggle from Elodie.

"I don't know. Winchester does have its charms."

As she reached for the plate of French toast, a loud knock echoed through the empty house, followed by the frantic ringing of the doorbell. Elodie frowned. "Are you expecting anyone?" she asked.

"No one knows that I'm here."

She jumped out of bed and searched the room for something to put on. When she picked up his cargo shorts and hitched them up on her waist, Dev had to chuckle. "Now that's a sexy look," he said.

"How small is your butt?" she asked. "These almost fit me. Clearly I need to go on a serious diet."

"Don't you dare," Dev said. "I like you exactly the way you are."

"Plump?" She hurried out of the room, and Dev listened to her footsteps as she descended the stairs to the foyer. He heard the creak of the front door and then a man's voice. Frowning, he pushed the breakfast tray aside and crawled out of bed, searching for something to wear. All she'd left him with was his boxers. He grabbed them from the floor and pulled them on.

A moment later, Kyle Dunphy peered around the bedroom door. "Hey, boss." He held out his hands. "Let me make something very clear. I can't see anything. I'm not making any snap judgments. I'm just here to deliver some information and then I'll get out of your way."

"This couldn't have waited?" Dev asked.

"I didn't think so. But I'll let you be the judge. By the way, we've been trying you at home and on the radio and we were all getting a little worried. It's half past ten and you're—"

"What? What time did you say it was?"

"Half past ten?"

"Sorry," he said. He glanced around. "Where are my clothes? I need my clothes."

"Let me just deliver my news and then I'll get lost," Kyle said. "I checked the registration on that gun that we pulled out of Jimmy Babcock's car. It came back as stolen."

"No surprise," Dev said.

"Except that it was stolen in that gun store burglary in Asheville last month. The one where they got away with nearly a quarter million dollars worth of guns and ammunition."

Dev cursed softly. "No wonder Jimmy's family is willing to hang him out on this one. At least we've eliminated his father. He's not smart enough to pull off a job like that. Ray and his crew could, though."

"Well, ATF is going to come calling, and if we don't want Jimmy swept along into this thing, you're going to need to convince him to tell you what he knows, and fast."

"All right. You go back to the station and see what you can get me on that gun store job. All the details. Before ATF gets hold of the gun, send it over to the county lab for fingerprints and DNA. And find Ray Don Babcock. I want to talk to him before the Feds do."

"I'll get right on it, boss."

Kyle turned to leave, but Dev stopped him. "How did you figure out I was here?"

The officer shrugged. "It's a small town, boss. It's kinda hard to keep anything a secret. There's been talk about you two since the moment she drove back into town. Lots of it is still speculation, but…"

"I trust you won't be adding to the gossip?" Dev asked.

"No, sir."

"Good. I'll see you back at the station."

With that, Kyle hurried down the stairs. Dev strode to the door and found Elodie waiting for him in the hallway. Her fingers played with the hem of his T-shirt. "I guess you're going to need your clothes?"

"Was it really necessary to show him to the bedroom? You could have come up here to get me."

"He said it was an emergency," Elodie murmured. "And he seemed to know you were here. He must be a very good detective."

"He's not a detective. Just a patrol officer. According to him, the whole town believes we're together."

"Is that good or bad?" she asked.

He shook his head. "That remains to be seen."

"You should probably go," she suggested.

He reached out and wrapped his arm around her waist, pulling her against him. "I don't want to go."

"I don't want you to, either," she said.

"Promise me we'll do this again?" Dev asked.

Elodie looked up and met his gaze. "I promise. Again and again and maybe again—if you're not too tired."

He brushed a kiss across her lips. "I need my clothes."

She tugged the T-shirt over her head, revealing the sweet curves of her body. He clenched his fingers, fists at his side, knowing that if he indulged in just one caress he might never leave. When she handed him the shorts, he quickly pulled them on over his boxers, then tugged the T-shirt over his head.

Now that he was fully dressed and she was completely naked, the thought of walking out was almost impossible to imagine. Though he was as loyal to the job as they came, there were moments when he wished he had more control over his time. "What are you going to do today?" Dev asked, swallowing hard.

Elodie turned and walked back to the bed, offering him a delightful view of her rear end. "I have some projects I'm working on. And I'm going to drive over to Rocky Point. They've got a small art museum that I wanted to tour."

Dev didn't want to leave without properly and thoroughly kissing her. But he knew he would only be delaying the inevitable. In the end, he reached for her hand and pulled it up to his lips, then pressed a kiss to her fingertips. "Last night was incredible. And I'm sorry I can't stay for breakfast—and lunch."

"And I'm sorry if I created any complications for you and your officer."

"I'll call you later?"

Elodie nodded. "I'll be here."

He left her in the bedroom, standing naked, her pale hair tumbling around her face in tangled waves. He had made her look that way, Dev mused. He'd mussed her hair and kissed her so hard her lips were slightly swollen. He'd made her heart race and her body ache. He'd brought her to release not once, but three times over the course of the night. He was responsible for that sweet, yet satisfied smile that curled the corners of her mouth.

He couldn't muster a single ounce of regret for what they'd shared. Hell, he didn't care if the whole town thought they were having an affair. He knew better than to try to stop the gossips. But he would take care not to give them more to talk about. He didn't want to make more trouble for Elodie.

So, to everyone else, he and Elodie would seem like good friends and old acquaintances, a couple of people who occasionally shared a dinner out or a drive through town. But that would all change in the quiet confines of her bedroom. There'd be no holding back for either of them, no worrying about appearances.

Dev slipped out the back door, then made his way through the tangled mess that was the garden. He jumped the fence and then skirted the edges of two more yards before coming out on Azalea Street.

Picking up his pace, he started to jog. But no matter how fast he ran, he wasn't going to outrun the feelings pulsing through him. He was falling in love with Elodie Winchester. And there was absolutely nothing he could do about it.

5

ELODIE HAD BEEN in town for just over a week, and though people seemed to recognize her, very few of the towns-folk greeted her on the street. In truth, she could count on one hand the people in Winchester who had been friendly to her—Dev, of course, and his mother. Joannie at the café now smiled when she stopped by for lunch. Officer Kyle seemed to accept her. And finally, Susanna Sylvestri, the glass artist who had replaced her windows. They'd had lunch the day before to talk about her work.

"Five friends," Elodie murmured. "In one week." Manhattan had been friendlier. But then, no one had known her there—or her family's reputation. Maybe she ought to consider five a good start. She'd simply have to change people's minds one person at a time—assuming she stayed, of course, which wasn't likely.

She had a nice life in Manhattan, a good job and a lovely group of friends. And though her apartment was the size of a closet, there were so many things she loved about the city.

And yet, when she was here, she felt like she had a purpose. She owed it to the house and to the town to see what she could do for them. Her plans might fail miserably, or she might be run out of town before she even got started, but she had to try.

She stopped in front of the office for the *Winchester Journal*. The paint was flaking off the front door and the blinds across the plate-glass window were faded, but the paper was still running. She'd read the latest issue over coffee at Zelda's just this morning.

Grabbing hold of the door, she pushed it open and stepped into the cool, dimly lit interior. Dust motes swirled through the shafts of sunshine coming through the blinds, and the scent of newsprint and fresh ink filled the air. It smelled exactly like the Sunday *New York Times*, Elodie mused.

"Can I help you?"

An elderly woman appeared from the back, wearing an ink-stained apron and gloves. She pulled off the gloves, shaking her head. "Damned press. One of these days, it's finally going to give up the ghost and I'm going to move to Florida and live with my sister. What can I do for you, dear?"

"I'm hoping you can help me—"

"Wait," she said, frowning. "Are you Elodie Winchester?"

"Yes," Elodie said. She held out her hand. "It's a pleasure to meet you…"

"Oh, I'm Violet Feeney. Editor and publisher of the *Winchester Journal*, serving Winchester and the surrounding area for over one hundred and twenty years. I haven't been here for that long, but the paper has."

"Well, you are exactly the person I'm looking for," Elodie said. "I'm working on a project and I'm hoping to find local folk artists who'd be interested in promoting their work. I read that article you ran on the quilters club in your last issue, and I thought you might be able to give me information on other artists."

"Artists?" she said. "I doubt those quilters consider themselves artists."

"Oh, but they are," Elodie said. "I believe they are."

"We do keep a clip file," she said. "Most papers index their content on a computer nowadays, but we're a little behind the times," Violet said. "Still do everything the old-fashioned way."

"Could I look at the clip file?" Elodie asked.

"Let me go fetch it for you," Violet said.

Violet cleared a table for Elodie in the rear of the shop and set down a pile of file folders. "If I can get you anything else, just give me a shout."

"Thank you."

Elodie picked up the first folder and flipped through it, scribbling down notes as she went along. Her plan was taking shape, a chance to help the people of Winchester and to draw tourists to the charming town. It would be a small start, but Elodie wanted to use her expertise to help.

After combing through articles from the past ten years, she felt as though she had a good group of artists to approach. She'd start by inviting them to a small reception at the Winchester mansion, where she would explain her plans for a folk art gallery right there on the first floor of the house. And then she'd host an art fair, hopefully spanning two or three blocks of Wisteria Street, featuring artists from all over North Carolina. And finally, she would explore her idea of turning the old mill into artists' lofts, combining both studio space and living accommodations for talented artists.

It was an ambitious plan, but Elodie had heard of similar projects in other states where they'd transformed failing industrial towns without hope into thriving artists' communities. Many had transformed old factories and mills into condo complexes or shopping malls, creating an interesting mix of history and commerce that always seemed to draw a tourist crowd.

Elodie had plenty of resources to draw upon. She'd made a lot of important contacts managing the gallery in Manhattan, clients who had money to dole out to worthy causes. Renovating the mansion for her own purposes was out of the question, but if she turned it into a nonprofit gallery to showcase local folk art, then more sources of funding would be open to her.

And what better way to kick off the fund-raising campaign than an art fair? She could just imagine the streets filled with artists' tents, the booths stuffed with interesting work.

Elodie stood up and gathered her things. Violet returned to the room, a box in her arms. "Finished with your work?" she asked.

"I am."

"I hope if you're planning something newsworthy, you'll come to me and let me put it in the paper."

"You'll be one of the first to know," Elodie said.

Violet held the box out to Elodie. "I thought you might like to look at this," she said. "There's so much here, I packed it up so you could take it home."

"What is it?"

"The history of your family here in Winchester," Violet said. "It's interesting reading." She chuckled. "You might want to start with your great-grandfather's feud with Chief Cassidy's great-grandfather. Back in the day, it turned this town inside out."

"Dev Cassidy?"

"Yes," Violet said.

"I've never heard anything about it," she said.

"Oh my, there were years of lawsuits. The Winchesters were a powerful family even then, and this Lochlan Quinn was just a worker in the mill. He came up with some kind of invention with the looms at the mill. Your grandfather stole the idea and made millions on it."

"When was this?"

"Long before you were born, my dear. Long before most people were born—there aren't many in town who still remember it. Your father was just a boy. It's all in there."

"Thank you," Elodie said.

"Just make sure you bring the clippings back when you're done," Violet said.

"I will," Elodie said. She picked up the box and followed Violet to the front door, then stepped outside into the midday heat. It was only then that she realized she'd walked downtown rather than taken her rental car. She wasn't prepared to carry the box all the way home. But the police station was only a block away. Maybe she could ask Dev to deliver the box to her that evening when they got together for dinner.

She turned toward the station, but as she was struggling with the heavy box, she heard the blast of a siren behind her. The sound startled her, and the box slipped from her hand and landed with a thud at her feet. Dev's police cruiser pulled up alongside her, and he smiled at her.

"Need some help?"

"You startled me," she said. "Aren't there rules for using that siren?"

"Yes," he said. "And trying to attract the attention of a beautiful woman is against the rules. Are you going to report me?"

She smiled and shook her head. "No. But only if you take this box and drive it to my house later for me. I walked downtown and it's too heavy to carry all the way home."

Dev hopped out of the car and crossed the distance between them, then picked up the box. "I'll take both of you home," he said. "Get in."

He put the box in the backseat, then held open the passenger side door for her. Elodie got inside and waited for Dev to get behind the wheel. When he did, she turned to him. "What do you know about your grandfather Lochlan Quinn?"

He frowned. "What?"

"Your grandfather. His name was Lochlan Quinn."

Dev shook his head. "I don't have a grandfather

named Quinn. At least, not one that I've ever met. My mom doesn't talk about her family. My dad walked out on her when I was just a baby, and both her parents were gone by then, as well. That's all I know about my family."

"Well, according to Violet from the newspaper office, your grandfather was a man named Quinn and at one time he worked for my grandfather."

He leaned over and brushed a kiss across her lips. "That's all very interesting. It seems everyone in this town worked for your family."

It was, Elodie thought. But she hesitated to tell him the bit about her grandfather allegedly stealing Lochlan Quinn's idea. To nearly everyone in town, the Winchesters were evil overloads, a power-hungry family that had made life miserable for everyone beneath them. Dev was the only friend she could truly depend upon. She didn't want to say anything that might change his mind.

"Do you have time for lunch?" Elodie asked. "We could stop by Zelda's and—"

"I can't," Dev said. "I'm due to appear in court at two."

"Jimmy?" she asked.

He nodded.

Dev had been working tirelessly all week to try to help the young man. Despite his efforts, Jimmy had been locked up in the county jail and given an impossibly high bail. Dev had been trying to get him out, but Jimmy was protecting his family, and his father and brother weren't talking.

"Is there anything I can do?" Elodie asked.

He sighed, then shook his head. "I wish I could get him to see what he's going to lose. He thinks he's being noble but he's just being stupid." Dev cursed softly. "What I'd really like to do is forget all of this for just one evening. There's a picnic in the park tonight to benefit the fire department. I have to go and it would be a lot more fun if you'd come with me."

"Would that be a good idea?" she asked. "I don't want to be the dark cloud that spoils everyone's fun."

"You'll be with me," he said. "No one will bother you."

Elodie considered his invitation for a long moment, then shook her head. "I think I'll pass. I have a lot of work to do. But why don't you come over afterward and we'll have a late dinner."

"When are you going to tell me about this project of yours?"

"When I get it all sorted out," she said.

Dev pulled up in front of the mansion, then hopped out of the cruiser and circled around to help her. He retrieved the box of clippings and walked with her up to the porch.

"So, I'll be back later tonight," he said.

Elodie smiled. "I'll see you then."

"Stay out of trouble," he warned.

"*You* stay out of trouble."

He pulled her into his arms and gave her a long, lingering kiss, his tongue teasing at hers. Elodie was tempted to pull him inside for something more intimate, but she wanted to wait until they had more time.

As Elodie watched him jog back to the police cruiser, she smiled to herself. For the first time in a very long while, she was utterly and completely happy. And Elodie suspected that it had everything to do with Dev Cassidy.

"B-SEVEN. B-SEVEN." Dev reached into the bin and pulled another bingo ball out. He'd agreed to call the big-money game in the bingo tent, and it was quite a change of atmosphere from the raucous party outside.

Every summer, Winchester's volunteer fire department sponsored a barbecue, an all-day and night affair in the town park, attended by nearly all of the town's three thousand residents. There were rides and games for the kids, food and dancing for the adults, and plenty to drink.

Dev glanced at his watch. It was nearly 9:00 p.m. Any minute now, he'd be called upon to break up the first of the evening's fights. Between now and closing time at eleven, he'd mediate arguments over sports, family, romance and who owned the best hound dog in the county. Occasionally, he'd make an arrest if the fight turned physical, but he hoped that there'd be nothing serious tonight.

"I-seventeen," he said. "I-seventeen. I've got a feeling there's a bingo coming up on this next number. Who's going to win this big pile of cash?"

He pulled another ball from the bin, but before he could read it, Eddie Grant from the grocery store hurried over. "Officer Kyle sent me in here to get you," Eddie said. "There's a problem outside."

"Can't he deal with it?" Dev asked.

"He thought you'd want to deal with it. It's Elodie Winchester."

"What about her?"

"She's here. And she's causing a bit of a stir."

Dev handed Eddie the next bingo ball. "Finish calling the game," he said. He jumped off the riser and hurried outside, following the sounds of shouts and jeers. He found a small crowd gathered near the games, and he pushed through to find Elodie caught in the center of it.

"What the hell is going on here?" Dev demanded.

"She has a lot of nerve showing up here," Jeb Baylor said.

"We don't want any Winchesters in this town," Art Holman added.

Hank Pearce pushed through the crowd, his face red with anger. "She's just a reminder of everything her old man stole from us."

"Go back to where you came from!" another man shouted.

"Get out of here. This isn't your town anymore," said Jeb.

Dev placed himself in between the drunken crowd and Elodie, but she pushed him aside. "I don't need your help," she murmured.

Elodie cleared her throat, then tipped up her chin defiantly. "I understand why you're angry. And I don't blame you. My father did horrible things in the name of profit. And since I'm the only Winchester in the vicinity, you can take it out on me. Who'd like to hit me?"

"Elodie!" Dev moved to stand in front of her, but she just pushed him away again.

Four or five of the men in the crowd raised their hands and she nodded. "All right. Each of you can take one punch."

A low murmur went through the crowd as the men moved forward. "Don't be ridiculous," Jeb Baylor said. "I'm not going to hit a woman."

"Slap me, then," Elodie offered. "I can take it."

"No!" Several of the women in the crowd began to protest, and before long the conflict had created two factions in the crowd.

"No, she *won't* take it," Dev shouted. "That would be assault. And I will arrest you, count on it."

"Not if she's asking for it," Frank Sinclair said.

"That's right," Elodie said.

"All of you, just move along," Dev said. "There will be no slapping or punching here." He bent close to Elodie. "We need to get you out of here right now." Dev slipped his arm around her waist.

"I'm not leaving," Elodie said. "We're going to get this sorted out tonight. Wait!" she called. "I have an idea. Follow me."

Dev held tight to her arm. "What are you doing?"

"You'll see."

Elodie stopped in front of the dunk tank, then faced the enemy. "I'll spend the rest of the evening in the dunk tank," she said. "If you want to take your chances, you can buy three balls and try to put me in."

This seemed to interest most of those who had gathered. "Yeah," Jeb said. "That'll work."

"Just one thing," she said. "Instead of a dollar for three balls, it's ten dollars. I understand the fire department needs a new pump truck and we can help make that happen."

"You don't have to do this," Dev said to her.

Elodie turned to him, grabbing his arm as she kicked off her sandals. "I'll be fine."

Dev watched as she crawled up the steps and then scooted out onto the rail.

"Ten dollars for three chances," she called to the attendant.

Within minutes there was a long line of both women and men waiting to take a shot and dunking her. Dev watched, his temper barely in check, furious that the whole town had ganged up on her.

"Folks are wonderin' where your loyalties lie."

Dev turned to find Frank Sinclair standing next to him, his angry gaze fixed on Elodie's slender figure.

"I'm responsible for the safety of everyone in town," Dev replied.

"I think you're concerned with a little more than her safety," Frank said.

Dev fought back a surge of anger. If he were any other man, he'd call Frank out and they'd end their disagreement with fists instead of words. But Dev was the police chief and had sworn an oath to promote harmony in the community. "You mind your own business, Frank, and I'll take care of mine."

"I'm just sayin' that if you side with the Winchesters, you might find yourself out of a job."

"Go ahead and try to fire me. I'm not worried. And

if it makes you feel like a man to dunk that nice lady in the tank, then you go right ahead. But don't be telling me how to do my job."

By the time the line at the dunk tank disappeared, the breeze had picked up and Elodie was shivering badly. Dev finally convinced her to come down off the tank, and he wrapped his arms around her and rubbed her back.

"Jesus, you're freezing."

Her teeth chattered and she forced a smile. "I'm just a little chilled."

Dev quickly escorted her to the cruiser. He found a thermal blanket in his first aid kit in the trunk, then wrapped her first in the silver film, then topped it with a rough wool blanket. "I'm taking you home."

They drove through the dark streets of Winchester. "You didn't have to do that, Elodie."

"Maybe I did," Elodie said. "They seem to want their pound of flesh, and if I want to live here even for a short while, I needed to give it to them. Even if it was with a silly dunk tank."

Dev glanced over at her. "Do you *want* to live here? I thought you were just going to stay until you sold the house?"

Elodie shrugged. "I'm not sure what I'm going to do. Staying here is one option. But if everyone in town hates me, that makes it a lot less appealing."

"Not everyone in town hates you," he said. "I feel very differently."

She chuckled softly. "Yes, and I'm glad. But you can't always come riding to my rescue every time someone is mean to me. And I know what our relationship is costing you. I don't want you to lose your job because of me."

"I won't," Dev said. "And if I do, then I'll just move on and find something else to do."

"And leave Winchester? You love this town. The people here need you."

They rode the rest of the way to the mansion in silence, their conversation at an impasse. Dev didn't want to admit that there might not be a future for them simply because of her last name.

"Are you hungry?" he asked.

"I'm just tired. And cold."

Dev pulled the car up to the curb and helped her out, wrapping his arm around her shoulder. "I'm going to run you a nice hot bath and then I'm going to make you dinner. And then we're going to crawl into bed and get a good night's sleep."

"Sleep? In bed?" she asked. "Now that's a novel idea."

ELODIE SANK DOWN into the warm water, her hair floating out on each side of her. She hadn't realized how cold she was until Dev stripped off her damp clothes and helped her into the tub. Now the heat was seeping into her flesh and making her feel sleepy and content.

"I brought you some wine."

She opened her eyes to see him standing in the bathroom doorway. Elodie held out her hand, and he slipped the glass between her fingers. "I'm exhausted."

"You should be. In and out of that tank for almost

two hours." He reached out and smoothed his hand over her cheek. "It was one of the bravest things I've ever seen."

"It was a dunk tank," she said. "I didn't swim the English Channel."

"You stood up to the town of Winchester," he said. "All by yourself. And I think you were right, it did some good."

"Did it?" Elodie asked. She couldn't help but smile. If anyone would know, it would be Dev. He understood this town better than anyone. "I'm lucky they had a dunk tank. I could have ended up in front of that dart game where they break the balloons. That would have hurt."

Dev laughed as he sat down next to the tub. He grabbed her wine and took a sip. "They admired you for what you did, stepping up and letting them blow off some steam."

"They probably still hate me."

"They probably do," Dev said. "But they might also respect you. And that's a step in the right direction." He paused. "Is it important that they like you?"

"Yes," she said. "It bothers me that my family name is viewed so negatively in this town. And I want to change that."

"Why? You're going to be gone as soon as you sell the house, aren't you?"

He was asking for the answer she hadn't given earlier. But she still couldn't give him the one he wanted. She sank down in the water and took a sip of her wine.

"I don't know. The more time I spend here, the less I want to go back to New York."

"It would be nice if you stayed," Dev said.

She glanced over at him. "Yeah?"

He nodded, then pushed to his feet. "And now that I'm aware you're considering that, I ought to do my best to convince you." Grabbing the hem of his shirt, he pulled it over his head.

Elodie watched as he slowly undressed. When he was naked, he stepped to the side of the tub.

"Are you going to join me?" she asked.

"Damn right," Dev said.

She moved forward, and Dev stepped in behind her, stretching his legs out on each side of her body. Elodie leaned back against his chest, and he wrapped his arms around her body.

"Now, this is the way to spend a Saturday night," he murmured, his breath soft against her ear.

"Have you done this before?"

"Never," Dev said. "I'm a shower kind of guy. Get in, get out, get to work. But now I see the allure."

"So you don't spend too many Saturday nights hanging out in bathtubs?"

He pressed a kiss to her shoulder. "I can't recall ever spending a Saturday night in a bathtub. How about you? If you were in New York, what would you be doing?"

"On a Saturday night?" Elodie considered her answer. In truth, she'd barely thought about New York since she'd left. Wasn't that some type of sign? If Manhattan were really home, wouldn't she be homesick?

"I'd probably attend a gallery opening or some charity event."

"Would you have a date?"

"I had a boyfriend. He'd come when he wasn't involved in a new project. He was an artist. And if he didn't go with me, I'd invite a friend. Or I'd go alone. Afterward, I'd have a late dinner. Now that I say it, it doesn't sound very exciting."

Her life had become a bit repetitive. What had once seemed exciting now bored her to death. But here, she had a fresh start, new objectives and an interesting man pursuing her. She had a purpose now. Her life didn't revolve around selling expensive paintings to very wealthy people.

She wanted to tell Dev about her plans, about her idea to open a gallery and host an art fair, even about the artists' colony in the old mill. But Elodie had never attempted anything of this scope and she still had a healthy level of self-doubt.

Everything revolved around her ability to raise money. Once she had her plans in order, she'd have to head back to New York and other places to secure funding. The thought of leaving Dev already brought pangs of loneliness.

But was she in love with Dev Cassidy? Now that was the question she needed to answer. She'd had other men in her life and had considered herself "in love." But this affair with Dev was different. Their time together ranged from the heights of desire to ordinary everyday events. And yet, every moment was as interesting and exciting as the last.

Elodie leaned forward and grabbed the washcloth, then squeezed water over her arms and shoulders. Dev reached out and gently massaged her shoulders. "This is heaven," she said.

"And you're an angel," he murmured.

Elodie giggled. "That was especially cheesy."

"I know," Dev said. "But I couldn't seem to help myself."

Elodie stood up and grabbed a towel from the shelf at the end of the tub. She turned and held it out to him. "The water is getting cold."

He stood, the water sluicing off his body. Elodie reached out and ran her hand over his chest, her fingertips skimming along the ridges of muscle and bone. Dev caught her fingers and pressed them to his lips.

A shiver skittered through her, and Dev frowned. "Still cold?"

Elodie shook her head. "No, not at all."

"Then what?"

"I think you better take me to bed."

Dev wrapped a towel around her body, then helped her out of the tub. They walked to the bedroom, their feet leaving wet tracks on the hardwood floors.

Dev gently pusher her down on the bed, pulled the towel away and tossed it aside. Then he knelt beside her and gently parted her legs. Elodie groaned, anticipating the pleasure that was about to come. Dev always seemed to know exactly what she needed, whether it be uncontrolled passion and fire, or a soft, sweet seduction.

When his tongue found its target, her body responded immediately, every nerve suddenly tingling with anticipation. She arched against him and focused on the sensations pulsing through her body.

There was nothing more in the world she could possibly want. At that moment, she was willing to give up food and water, creature comforts, just to experience that delicious climb toward her release.

But it wasn't just the physical that she craved. It was more than the slow build and the explosive ending. There was an emotional connection with Dev, a trust that he'd protect her, even in her most vulnerable state.

Tonight, he seemed to want to prolong her pleasure, and Elodie was at first happy to let him. But after a short time, she found herself desperate for relief. Furrowing her fingers through his hair, she held him close, silently pleading with him to end the torment.

Elodie whispered his name, and Dev finally relented, taking her over the edge and into oblivion. Her body writhed uncontrollably. She pushed him away, but he was determined to see her orgasm through to the final spasm.

When it was over, she opened her eyes and stared up at the ceiling. "You've wrecked me," she gasped.

"You're welcome," Dev replied. He crawled up and lay down beside her. "Is there anything else I can do for you?"

She was too exhausted to get up. "I could use something to eat. A piece of toast would be lovely."

Dev dropped a kiss on her lips. "Anything else?"

"Orange juice," she said.

When he left the room, Elodie crawled beneath the sheets and buried her face in the down pillows. A groan slipped from her lips. This was all happening so fast, and it was impossible to sort out her feelings.

At first, Dev had been just a piece of her past, a memory she wanted to revisit, a few moments she wanted to relive. But this passion between them had taken on a life of its own. She couldn't deny the power it held over them both. And it wasn't something to be casually tossed aside.

But her feelings for Dev were clouding her judgment. When she'd come to Winchester, it had only been to find a way to get rid of the house, to divest herself of the last bits of her childhood. But now she was searching for reasons to stay, rationalizing the need to build a life here in Winchester.

Did she really belong here? Was this the life she wanted? If she made the decision to stay, she had to be fully committed. The townspeople had been disappointed by the Winchester family in the past, and she wasn't going to do that to them again.

But what if this affair with Dev fizzled out? How could she live in Winchester if their relationship soured? And even if their passion lasted, it would be a long time before the town forgave her. They would punish him for her family's mistakes.

The solution was simple, Elodie realized. If she stayed, she'd have to end her affair with Dev.

6

ELODIE CHECKED THE address on the slip of paper, then drew a deep breath and knocked on the screen door. "Hello? Anyone home?"

A few seconds later an elderly woman appeared, her floral dress covered with an old-fashioned apron. "Hello there. You must be Elodie Winchester."

"I am. Are you Mrs. Clarkson?"

"I am. Come in, come in. I'm just taking some scones out of the oven and we'll have tea. How does that sound?"

"Lovely," Elodie said as she stepped through the door.

The tiny Cape Cod was awash with chintz and vintage bric-a-brac, so cozy and inviting. They walked through to the back patio where Mrs. Clarkson settled Elodie on a comfortable wicker chair on the back patio, then excused herself to fetch the tea.

Much as she feared that digging into the past could make things infinitely worse, Elodie had spent the past few days sorting through the clip file for the Winchester

Mill. If she was going to make things right in Winchester, she had to know what had been done wrong.

In the file, she had come across the name Jack Clarkson over and over again. Clarkson had been the attorney who had handled all the legal matters for the mill until 1990. She suspected he was one of the few remaining people who could shed some light on the fight between Dev's grandfather Lochlan Quinn and her grandfather. Had the Winchesters really cheated the man out of millions?

Her parents had always considered Mary and her son as part of the help, there to serve them. But had there once been a chance that Dev's family might have achieved the American dream, only to have it stolen away from them by her grandfather?

She needed to know the truth, though Elodie wasn't sure what she'd do with the truth once she had it. Was she ready to tell Dev that his mother might never have had to work as a maid? Or that he might have had the funds to go to a good college and find a life outside Winchester? Would he blame her, even though she hadn't even been born when it all happened?

Mrs. Clarkson returned a few minutes later with an old tea table and set it down in front of Elodie. She poured tea for them both, then placed a freshly baked scone on a plate and handed it to Elodie.

"Milk and lemon here," she said. "And butter and jam. My homemade peach preserves. Remind me to give you a jar before you leave."

"Is Mr. Clarkson going to join us?"

"Oh, dear. I guess I forgot to mention that Jack is not

very good with remembering things. He had a stroke a few years back and his long-term memory has never been the same. But I was his assistant for all the years he worked for the Winchesters. And I remember just fine."

"Do you remember Lochlan Quinn?" she asked.

"Oh, yes. Quite well."

"Tell me about him," she said.

"He came to Winchester after the war. He'd had some experience in textile mills in Ireland and England and he helped to install a new loom. He was a clever man and he helped your grandfather modernize the equipment in the mill."

"I was curious about the lawsuit," Elodie said.

"Oh, yes. As I remember, he developed some new system for threading the looms, some gadget that made the job quicker. He left it to your grandfather to take care of the patent, but when other mills wanted to buy the technology, he was frozen out of the profits. When he confronted your grandfather, he produced an agreement that any patents filed by Quinn while in the employ of Winchester Mills would belong to the mill."

"Had he signed that agreement?"

"Quinn claimed he never signed it. Never even saw the document. But the Winchesters were a powerful family. Quinn was a foreigner, an uneducated Irishman." She leaned close. "If you ask me, I believed him. So did my husband." She paused and sighed. "He and his wife, Frannie, fought that lawsuit for years. It bankrupted them. Lochlan disappeared in 1959. A lot of folks around here believed the Winchesters had something to do with his disappearance. Frannie died in 1970, leaving poor Mary an orphan at fifteen. The Winchesters took her in and she started working as a housekeeper for them a few years later. She married when she was in her midthirties, but her husband ran out on her shortly after Dev was born."

"Does Dev know all of this?"

"I'm not sure. Mary doesn't talk much about the past. I think she prefers to forget all the pain and heartache. I'm not even sure if she's aware of all the details. She's always been very beholden to the Winchesters for giving her a job and a place to live."

Elodie had never thought about the circumstances of Mary Cassidy's life and what had brought her to work in the Winchester household. But now that she did, the truth caused an uneasy ache in her stomach. Mary had been the one to suffer the most in all this, and the best her family could do was offer her a low-paying job as a domestic servant.

Elodie fought back a surge of tears. She really wanted to admire her father and her grandfather, but the more she learned about their practices, the less she wanted to claim them as blood relatives.

She chatted for another half hour with Mrs. Clarkson just to be polite, but Elodie needed to get away and process everything she'd learned. She made her excuses and thanked Mrs. Clarkson for the tea, then started toward the door. But the elderly woman stopped her.

"I can't believe I nearly forgot this," she said. "It came last month and I've been meaning to get it to Mary Cassidy. Someone looking for information about Lochlan Quinn."

"I can give it to her," Elodie said. "She works at the house four days a week."

"Oh, that's lovely. Please say hello to her for me. I hope she's doing well."

Elodie tucked the letter in her bag, then said her goodbyes. As she strolled down the sidewalk to the street, she drew a ragged breath and fought back another wave of tears. It was all so tragic—and unfair. Good fortune in life had nothing to do with luck or fate. It had to do with money and power.

Lochlan Quinn had had the chance to build a comfortable future for his family because of his clever mind. But the Winchesters had stolen that away from him, had denied him the wealth that could have changed the lives of his family, and instead they had continued to struggle.

Over the past few weeks, Elodie had been forced to examine her own feelings about her family's wealth. Though she'd had no hand in acquiring it, the effects of that wealth seemed to pervade her life. Maybe it was karma that her father had lost it all. Beyond paying his workers a wage, he'd never been a charitable or generous man. But Elodie had been unfazed by greed.

Here she was, trying to turn that old house into something wonderful and doing it on a dime. She'd been confident of her plans, but there was one thing that bothered her. The moment she made a success of something, her brothers would want a share. Though the house was technically hers, she knew that if they wanted it back, they'd find a way to snatch it out from under her.

Elodie got into her car and put the key into the ignition, then pulled the letter out of her bag. She shouldn't open it; it wasn't addressed to her. But what if the contents meant only more heartache for Dev and his family? They didn't deserve that. She couldn't change the past, but at least she could protect him from any future pain.

She unfolded it and scanned the text, then stopped and read more carefully. It was signed by a man named Ian Stephens who had been retained to find the family of Aileen Quinn. He was searching for information on Aileen's brother Lochlan, and had found the name in reference to a lawsuit filed in Winchester, North Carolina.

"Aileen Quinn," she murmured. "I know that name. How do I know that name?" She pulled her cell phone out of her bag and typed *Aileen Quinn* into a search engine, then waited for the results.

"'Aileen Quinn,'" she read. "'Born 1916, Cork, Ireland. Irish novelist.'"

Elodie skipped back to the search screen and read the next result. "Irish Author Seeks Missing Heirs. Gives Away Her Millions."

Now she remembered. She'd read a story in the *Times* literary section about this. The details were foggy in her mind, though, and when Elodie tried to find the article, she realized that her phone battery was nearly dead. She had her computer with her. A stop at the café for an iced tea and internet access was next on the agenda.

What were the chances that Dev Cassidy was one of Aileen Quinn's missing heirs? A hundred to one?

A thousand to one? Though Lochlan Quinn wasn't a common name in the United States, there were probably plenty by that name living in Ireland. And even if Dev was a descendant of the long-lost Lochlan, how would they prove it? The man had disappeared over fifty years ago.

Mary might know. But she still had to be cautious. She didn't want to give Mary and Dev false hope. She'd find out as much as she could on her own and then talk to Mary. Elodie drew a deep breath. Her family had taken away so much from the Quinns and the Cassidys. If she could make this happen for them, maybe she might be able to give something back.

DEV HADN'T BEEN sure he was going to make it through his shift. It wasn't difficult when he was busy, but on the days that he cruised around in his patrol car, he had plenty of time to think. And all he thought about was Elodie.

She'd become the center of his universe and though it felt wonderful to have her in his life, he also felt a measure of fear. How would he ever do without her if she left? Would he be able to resume his life as if nothing had happened? Or would he resign himself to being miserable for the rest of his days?

There was another option—leaving Winchester and following her wherever she went. But the thought of walking away from all the work that had to be done here was beyond impossible. He'd just have to enjoy what they had while they had it.

He reached up and brushed a strand of hair from her

face, taking in the sheer pleasure etched across her features as she moved above him. The dinner she'd been making was half-finished in the kitchen and the wine he'd brought along was sitting on the stairs, dropped there in their hasty charge toward her bedroom. There was only one hunger that needed to be sated at the end of the day and that was their desire for each other.

Dev smoothed his hands around her hips, slowing her pace for a moment. He'd become as familiar with her body as he was with his own. Dev knew how to touch her, how to make her writhe with pleasure before letting her surrender to her release. He'd explored every inch of her body with his fingertips, with his mouth. He'd caressed each curve, each angle, reveling in the scent of her flesh.

Now he leaned back, bracing himself with his hands as she sank down on top of him, wrapping her legs around his waist. Reaching out, he brushed a tangle of hair from her eyes and cupped her cheek with his palm. "I've been thinking about this all day long."

"All day?" she asked with a sleepy grin. "Every second of the day?"

"Almost," he murmured, nuzzling her neck. "I'd be driving around in my cruiser and I'd start imagining us, like this. I can't seem to stop myself. Will it ever stop?"

"Maybe you should see a doctor," she murmured. Elodie dropped a kiss on his lips, then traced a path from his chin to the middle of his chest.

She shifted above him, and Dev held his breath. He was buried deep inside her, and every tiny movement pushed him closer to the edge. It didn't take much, especially when he was with her like this, talking to her and touching her, staring into her eyes and memorizing her beautiful features.

He'd grown accustomed to all this. They spent every night together, their naked bodies tangled in damp sheets. And though he knew it could come to an end at any moment, Dev had refused to devote any thought to that possibility.

She hadn't talked about going back to New York, but then, she hadn't really committed to staying in Winchester, either. She'd said she was working on something, but had refused to tell him more until all the details were finalized. So Dev continued as he'd begun, happy just to have her in his life and unwilling to believe she'd ever leave.

Elodie leaned back and rolled her hips, her hair brushing against his thighs. A rush of sensation coursed through him, and Dev struggled to hold on to his control. "Don't move," he murmured.

She smiled seductively. "What do you want me to do then?" she asked.

"Touch yourself," he said.

"Is that all it will take?" she asked, her eyebrow rising quizzically.

"Tonight that's all it will take," he assured her.

She reached between them and began to stroke the damp slit with her fingertips. He watched as she began to lose herself to the pleasure. She closed her eyes and tipped her head back, her lips parted slightly as her breathing grew shallow and quick.

He felt her body tighten around him, and she moaned

softly. Dev reached out and cupped her breast with his palm, teasing at her nipple with his thumb. Elodie opened her eyes, meeting his gaze with a passion-glazed look.

He'd already been on the edge, and when her first spasm hit, Dev let her powerful release drive him into a deep and shattering orgasm, one that seemed to last forever.

She wrapped her arms around his neck and hugged him tight. "That was nice," she murmured.

"Now I have something new to dream about while patrolling the streets of Winchester," he teased.

"If people knew what you were really thinking about, the criminals would run amok."

"Hey, now, let's not go there. I've still manage to get the important things done. I finally convinced Jimmy Joe to testify against his brother."

"So he'll avoid a federal charge?"

"He should avoid all charges as long as he testifies."

Elodie gave him a quick kiss. "That's great."

"What did you do today? Besides think about me?"

She hesitated. "Actually, I was doing some research into your family," she said, her expression suddenly turning serious.

A stab of fear sliced through him at the sudden shift in her mood. "What?" he asked, turning her gaze back to his.

"How much do you know about them? Your mother's family and your father?"

Her question took him by surprise. "Not much, as I said earlier. My mother didn't have an easy childhood, and her parents died when she was young. She never talks about my father, and I don't blame her since he ran out on both of us." He paused. "I guess it really never made a difference to me." He took her hand and brought it to his lips. "Does it make a difference to you?"

"No," she said. "Well, not exactly. But there are some facts that you're missing. Kind of a good-news, bad-news thing." She winced. "What do you want first? The good or the bad?"

"How about neither," Dev suggested. "I really don't care about the past."

"But this is important to you now," she said. "So do you want to know how my grandfather swindled your grandfather out of millions? Or would you like to hear about how you might just be entitled to a million-dollar inheritance?"

"What are you talking about?" Dev asked. He sat up and crossed his legs in front of him, pulling the covers over them so they didn't get cold.

"I went to the newspaper office to do some research on my project."

"Your top-secret project," he said.

She smiled. "Yes. And while I was there, Violet gave me a big file of clippings about my family. She told me about a dispute between my grandfather and yours. His name was Lochlan Quinn and he invented this device to increase the efficiency of the looms at the mill. It ended up being quite important, worth millions."

"My grandfather was named Quinn? My mother's father?"

Elodie nodded. "Lochlan. He was from Ireland. Very

smart man. As the story goes, he left it to my grandfather to file the patent and my grandfather basically took all the profits for the invention from your grandfather. And now, your family officially has a reason to hate all the Winchesters."

Dev pulled her back down onto the bed and brought her body against his. Slowly, he ran his hands from her shoulders to the base of her spine. "Does this really make any difference?"

"You don't care that my family cheated your family out of millions?"

"Were you in on the scheme?" he asked.

"It happened before we were born," she replied.

"Then, no. I don't care."

Dev watched tears flood her eyes and he frowned. "What's wrong? Why are you crying?"

"I thought you'd hate me. I thought you'd be angry." She wrapped her arms around him and gave him a fierce hug. "You are the most decent man I've ever known."

"Sweetheart, it's going to take a lot more than your greedy relatives to make me hate you."

"What would it take?" she asked.

"I can't think of anything."

She nodded, relieved. "I'm glad," she said. "All right, now for the good news." Elodie crawled out of bed and crossed the room to her dresser, then returned with a small padded envelope. She pulled out a plastic tube and held it out to him.

Dev swallowed hard. What the hell was this? "Are you trying to tell me that you're pregnant?" he asked.

Elodie gasped and snatched back the tube. "No! I said I have that covered."

"Sure, but birth control doesn't always work and—"

"What if I was pregnant?" she asked. "What would you do? What would you say?" Elodie paused, then reached out and covered his mouth with her hand. "Never mind. We shouldn't speculate about such a thing. I'm not pregnant."

"So what is that?" he mumbled through her fingers.

"It's a DNA test."

"I'm confused," he said.

"Your grandfather Lochlan Quinn may be the brother of Aileen Quinn. She's a very famous Irish author who has been searching for the descendants of her four brothers. She was separated from them as an infant and now she wants to track them down and give their descendants some of her millions. If the DNA test proves that you're an heir and that your Lochlan is her Lochlan, you'll be entitled to an inheritance of about a million dollars."

"You're kidding, right? What's the punchline?"

Elodie shook her head. "Not kidding. This is real and there's a very good chance you're one of them."

Dev raked his hand through his hair as he stared at the DNA test. "What are the chances?"

"You won't know until you send this in," she said, waving the tube at him.

"She's just giving away money?"

Elodie nodded.

"All right, then I'm in." He grabbed her hand. "You're sure this isn't some kind of scam to steal my identity?"

"No," she said. "And there's one more thing. If you're related to Aileen Quinn, your mother is, as well, and she gets her share of the inheritance, too."

"Have you mentioned this to her?" Dev asked.

Elodie shook her head. "I was going to, but I wanted to wait until I had more information. And when you asked…I couldn't keep it from you any longer."

He flopped onto his back and stared up at the ceiling. "This is more exhausting than sex."

She propped herself up on an elbow to gaze down at him. "I know. But it's exciting, don't you think?"

He turned and looked at her. "Can we stop talking now and kiss?"

Elodie rolled on top of him, catching his hands and pinning them above his head. "Yes, we can. Would you like me to start?"

"Yes, please."

As she dropped kisses along his jawline, Dev sighed. He wasn't quite sure what all this meant. But a million dollars? That kind of money would go a long way to making a life for the two of them possible.

"WE HAVE THE sweets all laid out," Elodie said, "and the coffee is brewing. And thank you for the flowers, Mary. They really bring everything together."

"The table looks lovely, Miss Elodie."

The past week had been a rush of activity in the mansion on Wisteria Street. Elodie and Mary had planned an afternoon tea for twenty local artists. While Elodie had put together her presentation, Mary had baked red velvet cupcakes and lemon shortcake cookies. She'd made pralines and almond brittle and cute little tea sandwiches of ham and chicken salad.

They'd picked up a variety of mix-and-match china from a couple of thrift stores, along with some vintage glasses and goblets for the fresh limeade that Mary had also made. The event would be a simple tea, but Elodie didn't want to appear too pretentious.

"I just wish I'd had time to paint the walls," Elodie said. "The room would look so much nicer with a fresh coat of paint."

"These people are artists," Mary said. "They'll be able to see past all that to your idea. How could they say no?"

"They could easily say no," Elodie replied as she fussed with a stack of linen napkins. "Rehabilitating the Winchester name in this county will not be as simple as enjoying a glass of your famous fresh limeade."

"My limeade *is* very good," Mary said. She slipped her arm around Elodie's. "I have had fun doing this, Miss Elodie. And I hope that everything works out exactly as you've planned. I'd love for you to stay here. We could have tea like this every Friday afternoon."

Elodie slipped her arm around Mary's shoulders. "We've done our best. Now we just have to hope that the artists show up." She glanced at her watch. The afternoon tea was scheduled to start at 3:00 p.m. They had fifteen minutes to worry whether their invitation would be ignored.

She'd invited twenty local artists—painters, wood carvers, quilters, potters. She'd carefully studied their work, separating the artists from the craftsmen and searching for that certain something that elevated simple materials into serious art. For what she wanted to do, it would take a special mix of artists.

The doorbell rang, and Elodie smiled. "Someone is early. That's a good sign." She smoothed her hands over the skirt of her cotton dress, drew a deep breath and calmly walked to the front door. But when she opened the door, she didn't recognize the person on the other side.

"Miss Winchester?"

"Yes?"

"My name is Rhoda Merrill. I'm a real estate broker from Asheville. I have some clients who are looking for a house just like yours, and I was told that you've been trying to sell. I was just driving through town and thought I'd stop and talk to you."

"I really don't have time today, unfortunately," Elodie said. "I'm expecting guests in just a few minutes."

"Oh, I won't take much of your time at all. Would you mind if I walked through and got a sense of the place? I promise to keep from getting underfoot. And I'll be gone in ten minutes."

Elodie had given up on selling the house. In three years, no one had expressed an interest. But suddenly selling the house was back on the table. Should she cancel the tea? Or tell Rhoda the house was no longer for sale? Until she gave her presentation, she had no idea how her idea would be received. Best to keep selling as an option. "All right. But if you could go out the rear entrance when you're finished?"

The broker nodded and handed Elodie her business

card. "I'll stop by tomorrow, if that would be all right? We could talk a bit more."

"Fine," Elodie said.

"Would one p.m. work for you?"

"It would." Elodie stepped aside as she let Rhoda Merrill walk into the huge foyer.

"Oh my, this is lovely. Look at all this architectural detail. In so many instances, these things have been stripped away." She walked to the stairway and ran her hand over the banister. "Mahogany?"

"I believe so."

Rhoda wandered off into the rear of the house. "Can we trust her?" Mary asked, a suspicious arch to her brow.

"I'm afraid I don't have much of value to steal anymore," Elodie said. "Unless she plans to walk out with the light fixtures."

Mary's worries about the real estate broker were soon put aside as the first guest arrived, a potter from the nearby town of Croft River. Mary brought them both tea as Elodie chatted with her about the house and her experience selling folk art in New York.

To Elodie's relief, the front parlor of the mansion was soon buzzing with conversation as guest after guest arrived. Though the artists were curious about her plans, they were patient about hearing the details and instead enjoyed the opportunity to socialize. Finally, at quarter after the hour, Elodie decided that it was time to begin the presentation. Five of the twenty invited guests were missing, but fifteen was a good start.

Elodie moved to the front of the group and asked

for everyone's attention. Gathering her resolve, she explained her plans for a small gallery that focused on local folk art, plus an annual art fair for the town of Winchester and finally the possibility of artists' lofts in the old mill.

She was just getting to the heart of her speech, the point where she asked for their support, when the wail of police sirens filled the air. Distracted, her audience turned toward the windows, their gazes scanning the street through the curtains. Elodie tried to continue, but finally gave up and joined them at the windows.

A few seconds later, Dev burst through the front door and ran into the front parlor. He stopped short when he saw the group, his hand slowly sliding away from the holster of his gun. "I—I'm sorry. We got a call about a disturbance in the neighborhood."

Elodie pasted a smile on her face and hurried over to him. "No disturbance. Just afternoon tea."

Mary appeared at his side with a cup of tea, a shortbread cookie resting on the saucer. "Here," she said. "You look like you could use it."

Dev smiled at his mother. "Hi, Mom."

Mary shook her head. "Go ahead. Drink it. And pretend you're enjoying it. I won't have you ruin Miss Elodie's event."

"Event? Why am I the last person to hear about this event?" Dev whispered. "When we got a call about cars gathered on Wisteria Street, I assumed there was more trouble. What are all these people doing here?"

Elodie patted him on the arm. "Why don't you stick

around and listen to the rest of my presentation? Then you'll know everything."

He gave her a tight smile, then slowly made his way to the back of the room.

Elodie was surprised by his reaction. He seemed more irritated than curious. But it wasn't as if he told her every little detail about his professional life. And she'd had good reasons to keep this quiet. The entire scheme telegraphed her intention to stay in Winchester.

Though making the move back to her hometown had always been an option, it wasn't one she was willing to discuss with Dev. In truth, she wanted to make the decision without even considering the man who'd been spending every night in her bed, especially since she'd have to end their affair if she continued to live in town.

Making a move like this, leaving her career behind in New York, had to be based in something more than sexual desire and the need for a little passion in her life. Elodie was determined to take a logical, rational approach, weighing all the options without any interference from Dev. Yes, he was important to her, but their relationship could end at any time, and there were a lot of reasons why their relationship could never work.

Her presentation came to an end with a nice round of applause followed by fifteen minutes of questions. When she was finally free to socialize with the group, Dev grabbed her hand the pulled her toward the kitchen.

"I really should stay with my guests," Elodie protested.

"I just want a few minutes," Dev said.

Mary was in the kitchen, preparing another pot of

tea. When she saw Dev, she smiled, but he sent her a dark glare. "Why didn't you tell me about this, Mom?"

"Do you tell me everything that you do in the course of a day...or night?" she asked. Her meaning was crystal clear, and Elodie felt a blush warm her cheeks. She and Mary had never talked about the fact that she and Dev were lovers, though Elodie was certain Mary suspected what was going on.

"I'd like a moment alone with Elodie," Dev said.

Mary gathered up the plates on a tray and walked out of the kitchen. Dev turned to Elodie. "I'm sorry that I interrupted your...whatever this is."

"It's an afternoon tea," Elodie said. "And frankly, it was embarrassing. Don't you think you should have called me first?"

"You've had two incidents here. I wasn't about to take any chances," Dev countered. "Maybe if you'd *told* me about your afternoon tea, I wouldn't have rushed over here."

"So now it's my fault?" Elodie asked.

"I'm just saying that for a guy who's supposed to be important to you, I was surprisingly uninformed. This plan of yours for the gallery and the art fair—how long have you been working on it?"

"Almost since I arrived in Winchester," she said.

"And you didn't think it was important to mention it to me?"

Elodie felt her temper rise. He seemed determined to start an argument. And she was willing to give him one if that's what he wanted. "It doesn't have anything to do with you."

"Your decision to stay in Winchester doesn't have anything to do with me?" Dev shook his head, cursing softly. "I guess I have the answers I've been looking for."

"You're overreacting—"

"I have to go," he muttered. "Don't worry about me. I'm straight with it all. I was just...mistaken. You have a pleasant day, now, Miss Winchester." He put his cap on and strode out of the kitchen, the door swinging shut behind him.

She grabbed a shortbread cookie and threw it at the door. It shattered into a thousand crumbs as Elodie sank back against the edge of the counter. What did he want from her? They'd been together a couple of weeks, after years apart. She was having enough trouble sorting out a future for herself.

Did he really expect her to plan the rest of her life around him? Elodie drew a deep breath, then pushed away from the counter. There had been a time when Dev Cassidy *had* been at the beginning, middle and end of every one of her fantasies. But now that he'd become part of her reality, Elodie was forced to be practical. Her plan could fall apart. What if no one in the community wanted a folk art gallery on Wisteria Street or hated the idea of an art fair on a warm summer weekend? Maybe the people of Winchester would prefer that she left town quietly and never came back.

She'd hurt him once when she'd left, and she owed it to him to protect him from that kind of hurt again. She owed herself that, too. As long as she continued to think of their relationship as a vacation affair, then she could handle whatever happened.

The kitchen door swung open and Elodie held her breath, ready to face Dev again. But it was Mary who stepped through. "Is everything all right?" she asked.

"Where's Dev?"

"He left. Good thing, too. He was in a foul mood. I think we should serve the raspberry cordial now."

Mary had insisted they finish tea in the same way her grandmother used to—with a raspberry cordial that she'd made from an old family recipe. It was a silly nod to the past, but one she believed would appeal to her guests. "Right," Elodie murmured. "Let's do that."

7

DEV STOOD OUTSIDE the county courthouse, leaning against the front fender of his police cruiser. His gaze was fixed on the door leading in and out of the holding area, and he searched for a familiar face.

A few seconds later, Jimmy Joe Babcock emerged, squinting against the noonday sun. He glanced around, searching for a friend or family member, but after testifying against his brother on the gun possession charge, he'd been shunned by his family. His friends, those who hadn't sided with Ray Don, were in school.

Dev pushed away from the car and walked over to the kid. "I figured you could use a lift," he said.

"Thanks," he said with a hesitant smile. "I wasn't expecting Mom or Dad, but I thought one of my friends would come."

"I told them I'd come and get you. I stopped at your folks' house and picked up your clothes and your window-washing gear. You'll be staying with Coach Pembroke for now. He and his wife take in foster kids, and he agreed to give you a place to stay as long as you behave yourself."

"He's my history teacher," Jimmy said.

"Good. Then he can help you raise your history grade from a D to an A."

Jimmy frowned. "How did you know my—"

"I know everything about you," Dev said. "You are my current project. I've decided to do everything in my power to turn you into a cop. You'll start by finishing high school. Then, when you graduate, we're going to find you a good college and you're going to major in criminal justice. After that, I'll hire you on if you want to work in Winchester."

Jimmy chuckled. "You really think I could be a cop?"

"I do," Dev said. "Jimmy, you can do whatever you want with your life. Just because your name is Babcock, that doesn't mean your future is determined for you."

He turned away, but Dev could see tears swimming in his eyes. "My parents hate me. My brother is going to prison because of me and—"

"No," Dev said. "Your brother is going to prison because *he* decided to rip off that gun store. *He* decided to break his parole. He decided to leave that gun in a car that you drove and then was going to let you take the blame. He made all kinds of bad decisions before you had to make yours."

Dev reached out and put his arm around Jimmy's shoulders. "Come on. Let's get some lunch and then I'll take you over to meet Mrs. Pembroke. Then we need to stop at school and get all the homework you missed while you were sitting in that cell."

"I'll never catch up," he said.

"You will. After school, each day, you'll come over to the station and do your schoolwork until you have everything finished."

"Why are you being so nice to me?" Jimmy asked.

"'Cause I think you're a good guy," Dev said.

They started toward the car but Dev stopped when he heard a familiar voice calling his name. He turned to see Elodie approaching. Jimmy Joe glanced over at him, then whistled.

"You know her?" he asked.

"Yeah, I do."

He hadn't seen Elodie since their argument three days ago. He'd decided that he'd leave the entire thing up to her since she seemed to be the one firmly in control of her feelings. He'd been all-in from the start. But now that she was actually making plans to stay in Winchester, everything was starting to fall apart.

News of her plans had spread quickly around town, and within a few days two very distinct camps had developed—the pro-Elodie faction and the anti-Elodie group.

Her supporters felt that anything designed to bring tourists into town could only be positive for everyone living in Winchester. The "anti" group believed the town had to be completely Winchester-free in order for it to truly heal.

Dev wasn't sure which way the town council would go, especially since the issue was more emotional than practical. And Elodie needed the board on her side. In order for her to open the gallery, the council had to rezone her property as commercial. Since the mansion stood at the end of the street, it was unlikely that her neighbors would agree to the increased traffic. Elodie had a solution to that—she'd offered to build a new driveway through the back of her ten-acre property, coming off an already commercially zoned road. But that would also require a permit.

Dev didn't envy her the battle ahead, but she seemed perfectly willing to throw herself into it. He had to admire that about Elodie. She wouldn't take no for an answer. On the outside, she seemed sweet and soft, but that deceptive exterior hid a core that was as strong as steel. Dev just wished she was as determined to be with him.

Dev walked toward her, taking her hands as she pushed up on her toes and gave him a kiss on the cheek. He took the kiss as an olive branch.

"What are you doing here?" he asked.

"I had to pick up some tax information on the house," she said. "I have a real estate broker coming over this afternoon with a buyer."

Dev frowned. "I don't understand. You're thinking about selling?"

"I'm keeping all my options open," she said.

Dev had hoped that selling the mansion was the last of her options, not the first.

"What about you? Why are you here?"

"I'm picking up a friend of mine," Dev said. He motioned to Jimmy Joe. "Jimmy Joe Babcock, this is my friend Elodie Winchester. Elodie, this is Jimmy. Jimmy runs a window-washing business and Elodie owns a mansion with a lot of windows."

"Are you available?" Elodie said. "I haven't counted the windows, but there must be at least fifty. They haven't been washed for years."

Jimmy grinned. "I could come by and give you an estimate," he said. "I'll give you a good discount 'cause you're a friend of Chief Cassidy's."

"That would be fine," Elodie said. "I really have to go." She looked up at Dev. "I'll see you later?"

Was that a question, Dev wondered, or an invitation? He caught her hand and pulled her into a quick kiss. "Are we okay?"

She smiled and nodded her head. "I'm sorry about the other day. It's just that things are complicated right now. I'm trying to figure out what I want to do with my life."

"And I'm getting in the way?" Dev asked.

"No," she said. "Not at all. But you make it so easy to want to stay in Winchester, even if it might not be the right thing to do. I need to make these decisions with a clear head, and you have a way of muddling my brain until all I can think about is…you know. Maybe we should try to slow things down." She drew a ragged breath. "Can we do that?"

"We can," he said with a grin. "So, I'll see you around, Elodie."

"Definitely," she said.

He watched as she walked up the courthouse steps and disappeared inside. Dev sighed deeply.

"She your girlfriend?" Jimmy asked, stepping up beside him.

"I guess you could say that," Dev replied. "Though things are kind of messed up right now."

Jimmy Joe shook his head. "Man, you gotta lock that down. A girl like her, she's got her pick of guys."

"What do you suggest?" Dev asked.

"You gotta go exclusive," Jimmy said. "Forget playing the field. Once a girl as sweet as that walks, you'll never get her back. Like the song says, if you want it, you gotta put a ring on it."

"It?"

"Her," Jimmy clarified.

"So, you're saying I should formalize our relationship by buying her a diamond ring?"

"The bigger the rock, the better," Jimmy said. "So big that she can't possibly say no."

"I'm not sure that would be the right move. It might scare her off."

"Hmm," Jimmy said, reconsidering his advice. He frowned. "Well, if that's true, then she's kind of a weird chick. You'll have to take a different approach. If she isn't into material things, then she's probably all into emotions. Tell her how you feel. Reassure her that she's your boo."

"My boo?"

"Your bae."

"I can't believe I'm taking advice from a high schooler."

"You're, what, forty years old, and you don't have a woman in your life. Maybe you could use some good advice."

Dev reached out and ruffled Jimmy's hair. "I'm

twenty-nine," Dev said. "I'll be thirty next month. And I've had plenty of women in my life."

"Not like her," Jimmy said.

"All right, I'll give you that. Never like her."

Jimmy Joe patted Dev on the arm. "Why don't we grab ourselves a cold one and we can discuss this further?"

"Very funny," Dev said, giving the kid a playful shove. "And if I hear you've been out with those friends of yours stirring up trouble, I'll bring you right back here. Now is the time to take control of your life, Jimmy."

"Same for you," the boy said.

A TINY BEAD of sweat dripped down Elodie's cheek and fell with a plop onto her hand. She tipped her face up and ran the paint roller over the ceiling of the front parlor. She hadn't realized how grimy the paint was until she'd applied a fresh coat of white.

The house was stifling hot, the daytime temperatures topping ninety, and the humidity made it feel even worse. As she stood on a ladder just a few feet from the eleven-foot-high ceilings, the heat was practically unbearable.

She crawled down the ladder and placed the roller back into the pan. Elodie had hoped that one coat would be enough, but even now, before the paint was dry, she could tell it was going to require at least two.

Elodie wasn't sure why she was taking the time to paint. She hadn't decided to sell and she wasn't sure the gallery would be a go. Yet, she needed to find something to fill the void created by the absence of Dev. Up until a few days ago, she'd spent nearly every evening with him.

As she wandered back to the kitchen, Elodie tugged her T-shirt up and wiped her forehead. She found a bottle of water in the refrigerator and took it out onto the front porch. She poured half of it over her face, then took a long drink.

She drew a deep breath of the thick night air and closed her eyes. The silence made her ears ring. She'd been so used to the constant hum of the city while living in Manhattan, but here, it was so quiet, she could hear own heart beating.

The sound of a car caught her attention, and she watched from the shadows as a police cruiser slowly drove down Wisteria Street. Elodie held her breath as the car pulled to stop in front of her house. It had to be Dev. But instead of getting out, he sat in the car, the windows open, staring out the front windshield.

Elodie pushed to her feet and slowly walked down the porch steps. The bricks of the front walk were warm on her bare feet, as they'd held the heat from the day. By the time she'd reached the gate, Dev was out of the car, watching her across the roof.

"What are you doing out here?" she asked.

"Just checking out the residents on Wisteria Street," he said. "Normal rounds. What are you up to?"

"I was painting," she said.

"Oil or watercolor?" he asked.

"Latex. I was painting the ceiling."

"On a night like this? Too hot."

She smiled. "Being dropped into the dunk tank would feel good right about now. Or a long swim."

"You want to swim?" he asked. "I can make that happen."

Elodie hesitated before accepting. The last time she'd gone swimming with him, he'd stayed on shore, fully dressed, while she'd enjoyed the water. "I think Spencer's Landing will probably be crowded tonight."

"It is," he said. "I've chased kids out of there three times today already."

"Are you going to swim with me?" she asked.

"Sure. I'm off duty in three minutes. Come on, let's go."

Elodie shook her head. "I don't have a suit."

"You won't need one," he countered. "I know a place that's very private."

"I thought we weren't going to—"

"It's just a swim, Elodie, not a marriage proposal."

In truth, a swim sounded perfect right now. She could burn off the last of her nervous energy, cool down and then hopefully sleep like the dead. "All right," she said.

She jumped in the passenger side and they took off. Elodie expected that he'd head out of town, but instead, they ended up in the parking lot of the town's high school. Dev got out of the car and jogged around to help her out. The lot was empty, the windows of the school dark.

She got out and looked around. "How are we going to get in?"

"You're with the police chief," he said. "I have all kinds of access."

To Elodie's surprise, he unlocked a side door and they strolled inside. Dev took a flashlight off his utility belt to light the way as they walked through the empty hallways. When they reached the pool, Dev flipped on the underwater lights and the huge room suddenly glowed.

"Are you sure we're alone? There won't be a janitor happening by or a swim team dropping in for an unexpected practice?"

"It's a Sunday night. I come here all the time in the summer, often in the middle of the night if I can't sleep."

"All right. You first," she said.

Dev didn't hesitate. He stripped out of his clothes right there on the pool deck. He placed everything on a bench, and when he got down to his boxers, he turned and faced her. "I usually take it all off, but if you don't want me—"

"Go ahead," she said, nodding.

"I figured maybe because we'd decided to slow things down you'd—"

"Go ahead," Elodie repeated.

He hooked his thumbs in the waistband of his boxers and slid them down over his hips. Elodie groaned inwardly. If she had any sense left in her at all, she'd run the other way. This was exactly what she'd been trying to avoid.

But he'd said himself it was just a swim. Maybe she was the one reading too much into it. And if, by the end of the night, she and Dev were back in her bed, she had only one person to blame—herself.

Cursing beneath her breath, Elodie tried to appear

nonchalant as she tossed aside the shorts and T-shirt she wore. She reached behind her for the bra clasp, but Dev stepped up and slowly ran his hands over her shoulders. "I can do that," he murmured.

She didn't have the strength to stop him. The touch of his palms to her shoulders had already weakened her defenses. But after unhooking her bra, Dev didn't take it any further. Instead, he strode past her and dived into the deep end of the pool.

Elodie kicked off her bra and panties and followed him in, breaking the surface just a few feet away from where he did. Dev grinned at her. "See? That wasn't so difficult."

Treading water, she tipped her head back and sighed. "I remember Winchester summers being hot, but how did we ever do without air-conditioning? My father refused to put it in the house. He thought it was a sign of weakness. I think he didn't do it because if he installed air-conditioning in the house, the town would want him to air-condition the mill, too."

"I can't believe we're talking about the weather," Dev teased. "Things have fallen apart, haven't they?"

Elodie met his gaze. "Please don't say that."

"Isn't it the truth?"

"No."

"Then why are we naked with four feet of space between us?" He reached out, and Elodie laced her fingers through his. Dev pulled her through the water until their bodies touched.

Her pulse leaped, and her heart began to pound in her chest. Elodie looked down as his fingertips began to trace a line across the top of her breast. Just that contact, the bold caress, and she was aching for more.

His hand dropped lower, then cupped her breast, his thumb teasing at the hard nipple. A wave of exquisite sensation raced through her body.

Gathering her resolve, she pushed away and swam to the other side of the pool. "I could lose myself in you," she murmured. "It would be so easy. As simple as breathing."

"Then do it," Dev challenged. "Why spend the time we have together denying what we both want?"

"I'm trying to stand up here, all on my own, and you're like an earthquake, shifting the earth beneath my feet, throwing me off balance." She drew a ragged breath. "Why are you trying to make this more difficult?"

"I'm not," Dev said. "I won't. I can't apologize for wanting you or needing you. Besides, why are you so fixated on the future? Why can't we just live in the present and forget about what might happen tomorrow or next month or next year?"

"You make it sound so simple," Elodie said.

"Isn't it?"

She sank down in the water and watched him, silently observing the play of emotion in his expression. "Then you would be all right if this didn't work out and I went back to New York? You'd have no regrets? It wouldn't hurt you?"

"Not if we'd spent every last moment we had together making each other happy. I could say goodbye without a single regret."

"What if I couldn't?" Elodie asked. "It was hard enough to get over you when I was a teenager."

"Do you want me to convince you?" Dev asked as he swam closer.

Elodie shook her head. The look in his eyes sent a frisson of pleasure coursing through her body. Raw need. Uncontrolled desire.

She couldn't fight him any longer. Saying goodbye to him was going to hurt no matter what. So she'd take his lead and stop worrying about the future, at least for tonight.

THE MOMENT THE screen door slammed behind him, he gathered her into his arms and kissed her. His fingers tangled in her wet hair, and he tasted chlorine from the pool on her skin. Dev was like a man frantic for food and water—only his nourishment was Elodie's lithe, supple body.

It had taken a bit of convincing to get her to undress at the pool, but now she tore at her clothes, desperate to feel her skin against his. He hadn't bothered with his shirt after the pool. And when she reached for the waistband of his shorts, he skimmed off the bottom half of his uniform in one quick motion.

She reached for him, wrapping her fingers around his hard shaft, gently stroking him until he was completely erect. "Here?" he murmured.

"No," she said. She drew him along the corridor, and Dev expected to end up in her bedroom, but instead they ended up in the dark kitchen. He ran his hand over the surface of the kitchen island and smiled. The stainless steel was cool to the touch.

He spanned her waist with his hands and picked her up, setting her on the edge of the counter, and she lay back. He parted her legs and drove into her in one powerful motion, then paused, enjoying the feel of her warm body enveloping his shaft. Elodie cried out in surprise, a gasp slipping from her lips.

Then he started to move. It was rough and it was frantic, but that didn't stop either one of them. She reacted to each thrust, urging him on, demanding every last ounce of his attention.

Dev tried to focus on something besides the naked, writhing body laid out in front of him, but it was impossible. His self-control had vanished somewhere around the front walk to her house. He tried to slow down, but Elodie wouldn't let him. She sat up and wrapped her legs around his waist, slowly moving up and down along his shaft at will.

Again and again, she edged him closer to his release, then drew away. He knew she was close, too, her body sticky with sweat, her breath coming in quick gasps. But then suddenly, she drew back and crawled to the center of the island, giving him a predatory look.

"I'm hungry," she said.

"You want to eat in the middle of all this?" Dev chuckled, but she seemed dead serious.

Elodie eased herself off the other side of the island and walked to the refrigerator, then pulled open the freezer door. She withdrew a container and walked over to him, then pressed the freezing plastic against his belly.

He gasped at the sensation. "What are you doing?"

Elodie smiled. "Getting something to eat."

She opened the container, and Dev could see it was filled with strawberry ice cream. Reaching inside, she dug out a glob with her fingers and began to smear it across Dev's chest.

She pushed him backward until he came to a stop against the edge of the counter, and she slowly began to lick the ice cream off his chest. Her tongue was warm, branding his cold skin as she moved from one nipple to the next. His fingers tangled in her damp hair, and Dev was stunned by the erotic scene unfolding in front of him. Usually foreplay came before sex, not after it. But this change of agenda was definitely working for him—until she got out the blindfold.

It wasn't actually a blindfold, but a thin cotton dish towel. She picked it out of a drawer and secured it around his eyes then left him standing in the middle of the kitchen. He felt Elodie circling around him, her body brushing against his. He reached for her but she evaded his grasp.

"You're not going to let me touch you?" he murmured.

"No. But you can taste me." She guided him to her left breast, and he found the nipple covered with strawberry ice cream. He sighed softly, drawing the stiff nub into his mouth. He found the same treat on her right nipple and then followed a trail of ice cream down the center of her belly.

He set her on the edge of the counter again and knelt down, finding the sensitive spot between her legs. Without using his hands, he began to tease her with his tongue. Dev knew she was watching him, deriving her own pleasure from the sight of his seduction.

But because he was blindfolded, he was forced to imagine the scene. Every move flashed an image in his head that was wildly erotic. It was a strange, tantalizing experience, like nothing he'd ever done before. And he found himself caught up in the overwhelming passion his imagination evoked.

The pleasure continued for another hour, sometimes with the blindfold off, sometimes with the blindfold on. They each took turns tasting and touching the other. Dev had never enjoyed such a long path to release. In truth, he wasn't sure what to expect when the moment finally came to surrender.

He finally found himself deep within her heat again, Elodie's body soft and pliable after multiple orgasms. He stroked slowly at first, running his hands over her hips as she lay across the counter. He reached between her legs, determined to bring her to the edge once more. She shuddered once, and when he felt her come, Dev let go.

Wave after wave of pleasure washed over his body, the orgasm so powerful it made his knees buckle and his body spasm uncontrollably. It seemed to go on forever, and Dev rode it out until the very end, until he was drenched with sweat and completely spent.

He bent over Elodie and dropped a kiss on her lips. "Is there room up there for me?"

"Hmm," she said. "Plenty."

He crawled up beside her and lay back on the cool steel, staring up at the ceiling in the dim light. "This is now my favorite spot in the house," he said.

"What was your previous favorite spot?" she asked.

"Your bed. I liked your bathtub, too. And the front porch. But this is my favorite now. I could live here."

Elodie giggled.

"What?" he asked.

"I'm not sure your mother would appreciate your naked, sweaty body on her clean kitchen counter."

Dev groaned, rolling over to face her. "Did you have to bring my mother into this?"

"Sorry. But we will have to clean up the evidence of our night together before she arrives in the morning."

He sat up, pulling her along with him. "I need something to drink. How about you?"

"There's beer in the fridge. And iced tea and limeade."

Dev got up and grabbed a beer, then poured a glass of iced tea for Elodie. He leaned against the counter as he took a long swallow of the beer, content with his lot in life. He had Elodie back, at least for the near future. The passion was still blazing between them and nothing would change that.

They'd grown so comfortable with each other that even this seemed natural—the two of them, naked, lying across the kitchen island drinking a cool beverage on a hot summer night. Dev leaned forward and brushed a kiss across her lips. "Tomorrow night is the zoning meeting," he said. "Are you ready?"

She shrugged. "I guess so. There won't be much to it. I'll give them my proposal and they'll vote on it. If they vote no, there's an appeal process that I can go through, but I have a really good proposal. And by putting in the new driveway and a parking lot in the rear of the house, there won't be any disturbance to the residents on Wisteria Street."

Dev wasn't sure he should tell her the truth, that things wouldn't be as simple as she thought. They'd put their relationship back on track and he didn't want to spoil it. But he wanted to prepare Elodie for the fight ahead. He was the only one who could help her.

"Ellie, maybe we should go over your presentation. It wouldn't hurt. I'm familiar with the guys on the board. I know what kind of questions they're going to ask."

"It's not a big deal," she said.

He grabbed her hand and laced her fingers through his. "It is a big deal. There are people in town who don't want you here and they're going to do everything they can to get you to leave. They'll bring their complaints to this meeting."

"And where do you stand?" she asked in a quiet voice.

"You know where I stand. With you, all the way. I'll be at the meeting to keep the peace. It's liable to get a little rowdy. Just be prepared."

A worried expression settled on her pretty face, and Dev regretted even bringing the matter up. She had no idea how intense this meeting could become.

Elodie sat up and then slid off the counter. "I'm going

to go take a cool bath and then go to bed. Are you coming with me?"

Dev nodded. "I'll be up in a few minutes."

She walked out of the kitchen, clutching her iced tea glass in her hand.

Dev sighed softly. He wanted to protect her from anyone or anything that would hurt her. But she'd made it clear that she wanted to do this on her own. So this was one time when he'd have to stand back and let the events play out.

Tomorrow, the town council of Winchester would determine his entire future. It would decide whether Elodie made a home in town or left the next day. All he could do was hope they made the right decision.

8

"THIS MEETING OF the Winchester Town Council will come to order." The sharp rap of a gavel on wood brought the room to silence. Elodie glanced around the gallery of the old courtroom and tried to calm her runaway nerves. She spotted some familiar faces—Joannie from the café and Susanna, the glass artist who had fixed her window. Even Jimmy Joe had turned up for the proceedings.

Elodie caught sight of Dev standing at the rear of the room. Instead of his casual summer uniform, he was dressed in finely pressed khaki, his badge on display on his chest, his gun holstered at his hip. When he saw her, he gave her a thumbs-up. But he didn't smile. In truth, his expression was downright grim—matching many of the council members' expressions.

Had her fate already been decided in some back room? Were they just here to deliver the bad news and then move on to a discussion of garbage trucks or potholes? Maybe she was expected to pay a bribe for a favorable decision. Was that the way things worked in Winchester?

Elodie wouldn't be surprised. It was certainly the way her father had worked, and until recently, her father *had been* Winchester. Though the townspeople elected the council to represent them, its members had always deferred to her father on any decisions that affected the mill or his millions.

"Come to order. I'm Irv Solomon, president of the council, and I'll be running this meeting. I'm warning you now, if there's any trouble here tonight, I'll have you tossed out. Chief Cassidy is here and he's not afraid to make arrests if the behavior warrants." Solomon eyed the crowd, then continued. "The agenda was published in the paper, but since most, if not all of you, are here about the Elodie Winchester proposal, I move that we table other business and get right to her presentation. Miss Winchester, why don't you step to the podium and address the council. After you're finished, we'll take questions and comments from the public before we make our decision."

"Thank you," Elodie murmured. "So, shall I begin?"

A man stood up and shouted, "We don't want any Winchesters here no more. They're all thieves and grifters. As far as I'm concerned, we ought to be changing the name of the town and put her and the rest of her people in the rearview mirror."

A woman stood up. "I second the motion. Those who agree say 'aye.'"

"That isn't a proper motion," Solomon said, banging

his gavel. "You'll be allowed to speak *after* Miss Winchester is finished. Now, you all sit down and shut up."

The half of the audience standing reluctantly took their seats, but that didn't lessen the grumbling and whispering.

Elodie took a deep breath and began to explain the importance of the Winchester mansion to the history of the town. She admitted that her father had ruined her family's reputation and had caused many people harm, but she hoped to make up for what he had done with the gallery. She argued her plan would help promote local artists as well as draw tourists to town.

She talked about the art fair that the gallery would sponsor every year, and the possibility of redeveloping the old mill into shops and artists' lofts. She cited examples from other towns where a similar idea had worked. By the end, Elodie was satisfied she'd done her best to convince the townspeople that art was powerful enough to bring Winchester back to its former glory.

Elodie gathered up her papers and sat down, her gaze scanning the council for the members' reactions. Not one person in the group of seven was smiling. Elodie quickly stood. "I'd be happy to answer any of your questions."

Unfortunately, no one had any questions. There were, however, plenty of grudges and resentments and accusations that some of the townsfolk wanted to share. Elodie sat quietly and listened, but as the meeting dragged out, her patience was beginning to wear thin.

Tears pressed at the corners of her eyes, threatening to spill over in front of everyone, and it took every ounce of her determination to fight them off. Finally, she heard a familiar voice at the microphone and she turned to see Dev standing at the podium.

The crowd grew silent, and Dev cleared his throat. "Now that you've all off-loaded your old baggage, I'd like to speak for Elodie Winchester. She came back to this town without any expectations. But when she got here, she realized there was a way she could contribute, a way she could make our lives better. I know you're all still angry, but Elodie wasn't even living in Winchester when all that happened. Is it really fair to blame her?"

A few voices shouted "no" and Elodie smiled.

"Don't you think your opinion might be a bit slanted, Chief?" another person shouted. "You *are* sleeping with the woman."

That caused quite a stir, and Elodie felt her cheeks flush with embarrassment.

"I have something to say." Jimmy Joe Babcock stepped up to the microphone, and Dev patted him on the back. "Miss Winchester is good people. I'm an independent businessman and she hired me to do some work around the mansion. And isn't that what we all want—more jobs? People are going to have to work to make her plans happen. And I wouldn't mind having a share of that."

"She gave me a job, too." Susanna Sylvestri spoke up from the back. "And with a gallery to show my work, I'll be able to make a better living. Jimmy Joe is right, that's what we all want."

A few more people stood up to speak for her—Joanie from the café and Jeb Baylor's wife. In the end, the council decided to table the decision for two weeks in order to study her proposal more closely.

"When we come to a decision, Miss Winchester, we'll let you know," Solomon said and rapped his gavel.

As Elodie walked out of the town hall, she couldn't help but feel defeated. She'd spent so much time getting every detail of her proposal right, but none of it had made any difference. This decision would be a referendum on the Winchester family.

When she reached the street, Elodie couldn't hold back her emotions anymore. The tears overwhelmed her and she brushed them away with an angry curse. What the hell did she care what these people thought of her? She didn't need them!

"Ellie! Wait up!"

Elodie glanced over her shoulder to see Dev approaching and she sped up her pace. "Go away," she cried. "Leave me alone!"

"Elodie, come on." He finally reached her side and grabbed her arm, pulling her to a stop. "It's not over. They haven't made their decision yet. I understand how difficult that was for you to just sit there and take all that crap. I'm not sure I could have done it with such grace and dignity."

"I'm not sure why I bothered," Elodie said. "I should just sell the damn house and be done with it. Someone else can live in this hateful town."

"The buyers...they made an offer?" Dev asked.

"Yes, they made a formal offer late this evening. It isn't close to the asking price, but it's enough," she murmured. "I could walk away and never look back."

He reached out and cupped her cheek in his palm, turning her face up to his. "Is that what you want? Really?"

"No," she said. "I mean, not for us. But I don't know whether I have the strength to fight everyone's hatred and anger, and I don't want them to focus it on you. I don't belong here." She drew a ragged breath. "You do."

"We can change their minds," he insisted. "You just have to give everyone a little more time. I swear, they'll listen to me."

Elodie shook her head. "Or they'll start attacking you next. No. I don't want you riding in to save the day like some white knight."

"You aren't going to accept help, then? Why is my help worth less than what you'd get from anyone else?"

Elodie could see that he'd misunderstood. But she didn't know how to explain. She just needed to do this on her own, without Dev's interference. Sure, he might be able to change their behavior, but he'd never really change what was in their hearts.

"I'll wait to hear the decision, but if it's negative, I'm going to sell the house and leave," Elodie said.

"You won't appeal?"

She shook her head.

"And what if I find out I'm a Quinn?" he said softly. "What will that mean for us?"

Elodie laughed. "Wouldn't that be an ironic shift of fortunes."

"We wouldn't have to change the mansion into a gallery. We could live in the house and set up the gallery downtown, in one of the empty shops. Or at the mill. You have other options."

"But those take money," she said.

"Which I have. Or will, if the DNA comes out as we believe it will."

"You can't use your money on me. I won't let you. You could find a place away from here."

"Is it so bad that I want to find a place for the both of us? We could take that money and build a brand-new life. I could come to New York. Or you could come here. Or we could both move to Tasmania."

Elodie forced a smile as she backed away. "We'll talk about it later. I promise. I just have so much to sort through. I'll call you for breakfast." She hurried down the street, her heels clicking on the sidewalk. How was she expected to decide the rest of her life while standing outside the Winchester town hall? She needed time and distance, and she wasn't going to find either here in Winchester.

DEV SIPPED AT his coffee—his third cup that morning. He pretended to read the newspaper spread in front of him, but his mind was on the events of the previous evening. He wondered how Elodie was feeling. She'd broken her promise to call him for breakfast. It was nearly eleven and he had been wasting his morning waiting around for her call.

"That was quite a meeting last night. I felt a bit sorry for Elodie. I don't know how she kept it together through it all," said Joanie.

"She's a pretty amazing woman," Dev admitted.

"Last night was proof of that. I just wish the council would have made their decision last night. It isn't fair that she has to wait."

Joanie nodded. "I think that was more about crowd control than Elodie's project." She paused, then cursed beneath her breath. "I'm not really sure I should be telling you this but..."

"What?" Dev asked.

"They've already made their decision. They made it last night. They just didn't want to announce it with the crowd there."

"She didn't get it?"

Joanie shook her head. "It was a unanimous vote. Dev, you have to remember, most of those guys worked at the factory."

"So it was just retribution?"

"Pretty much," Joanie said. "What can you expect?"

"I guess I expected them to give her a fair shake." Dev cursed softly. "Now, I'm going to have to tell her."

"Or not," Joanie said. "If I were you, I'd approach each of those guys separately and try to convince them to change their mind. And once you had their votes, I'd urge Elodie to appeal."

"And what if I can't get them to change their minds?"

Joanie shrugged. "Is it really necessary to turn the house into a gallery? There's shop space downtown. Plenty to choose from. And what about the old mill? That's already zoned commercial."

Dev's radio squawked and he plucked it off his belt and answered. "Yeah, Sally. What's up?"

"I've got a gentleman here at the station who insists on seeing you. When are you going to be coming in?"

"I don't have time this morning. Tell him to make an appointment for next week."

"But, boss, he says he's come all the way from—"

"Sorry, Sally. I'm just too busy today." He signed off, then gulped down the rest of his coffee. "Keep that news to yourself," he said. "I'm going to try changing some minds before I say anything to Elodie."

"You really love her, don't you?" Joanie said.

Her statement caught him by surprise, but then, Dev realized the truth in it. He was working so hard to keep her in Winchester because he loved Elodie. He'd started loving her when he was a kid and now it had come full circle.

"I do," Dev said.

"Have you told her?"

He shook his head. "That would be the one sure way of getting her to leave town."

"I'm not so sure," Joanie said. "She looks like the kind of girl who has been dragging around a rather large torch. She might be in love with you."

"She'd tell me if she was," he said. "Elodie is always up-front about how she feels." Her honesty was one of the qualities that Dev respected most in Elodie. But it had also been the most difficult for him to handle.

She'd been clear that she wanted distance, and he hated to let that happen. But he understood that Elodie needed to make the decision to stay or return to New York without any consideration of what they'd shared.

"No," Dev murmured. "I'm pretty sure she doesn't

love me." He drew a deep breath. "I have to go. I'll see you later."

"If you run into Elodie, let her know that there's a small group of us here in town who support her idea."

"I will," Dev said.

He walked out of the coffee shop into the blazing noonday sun. The temperature was hovering around eighty, but there was a nice breeze blowing over the Blue Ridge Mountains that hinted of an afternoon thunderstorm. Dev hopped in his cruiser and turned around, heading the car toward Elodie's place.

He needed to be certain that Elodie was still determined to make her plan work. Joanie did have a point. If Elodie couldn't get the zoning variance, why not consider relocating the gallery? She could sell the house and still stay in Winchester.

Dev pulled the car up to the curb, noticing another vehicle with rental plates parked in front of the gate. Elodie had mentioned a buyer for the house. She couldn't have made that decision already, could she? Dev jogged up the front walk. He could hear voices inside as he rapped on the screen door. A few seconds later, Elodie appeared at the door, pale and flustered. "Dev! Oh, thank God you're here. I just called the station and—"

Dev's radio squawked and he grabbed it. "Boss, you better get over to the Winchester mansion. Elodie called and she said it was an emergency."

"I'm already here," Dev said. He met Elodie's gaze. "What's happening?"

"It's your mother," she said. "She needs you."

Dev pushed past her and found Mary sitting primly

in a chair, a dark-haired man standing nearby. Her eyes were filled with tears and she held a piece of paper and stared at it.

"Mom?"

"Oh, Dev! Look, look. You have to tell me if this is real. This man, Mr. Stephens, just gave me a check for almost five hundred thousand dollars. He says it's an inheritance, because my father was the—the—" She turned to the man and gave him an apologetic smile. "I'm sorry. I don't recall the particulars. Could you explain again?"

"Mr. Cassidy, I'm Ian Stephens. I represent the Irish author Aileen Quinn. You recently sent in a DNA sample and the test confirmed that you and your mother are both descendants of Lochlan Quinn, Aileen's older brother. As part of Aileen's family, you are also due your share of her considerable estate."

"But you say she isn't dead?" Mary asked. "That she wants us to visit her in Ireland. Do you hear that, Dev? Ireland."

Dev crossed the room and slipped his arm around his mother's waist. "Are you all right?"

"Just a bit taken aback, dear. Do you think he's telling the truth? Am I rich?"

"Here's all the paperwork," Ian said. "Along with a letter from Aileen inviting you and your mother to stay with her in Ireland as soon as you can make arrangements for the trip."

"She's just giving all this money away to complete strangers?" Dev asked.

"Not entirely. In order for you to collect the other

half, you'll need to pay her a visit. She's determined to meet every last descendant of her four older brothers."

Dev frowned. "What brought you here to the Winchester house?" Dev asked.

"You weren't available and your dispatcher gave me the location of your mother's workplace, so I thought I'd start here. I do hope you don't mind."

"No, of course not," Dev said.

Ian glanced around the room, then grabbed his briefcase and coat. "I'll let you two discuss this, let it sink in. I'd like to meet again at your convenience so I can answer any questions you may have. Perhaps we could make arrangements for the trip to Ireland. Miss Quinn is getting on in years and we never want to keep her waiting. Perhaps lunch at some point this week?"

"Lunch would be lovely," Mary said.

Elodie showed Ian to the front door. When she returned, her eyes were bright with excitement. "Can you believe it? He just showed up at the door. Like Publishers Clearing House."

Elodie hugged Mary. "I'm so happy for you." She turned to Dev and wrapped her arms around his neck. "And you, too. I can't think of anyone who deserves it more."

Some of the shock and suspicion had worn off, and Dev grabbed Elodie's waist and picked her up off the ground, kissing her thoroughly. When he set her down, her face was flushed.

"Congratulations." She stepped back. "Now, I do believe I have a bottle of champagne in the fridge. We should celebrate!"

Dev drew his mother over to the window seat set into the big bay window. "You're shaking," he said. "Sit. Relax."

"Do you understand what this means, Dev? I don't have to work. I can buy anything I need. I could buy a little house. Or maybe start a business. I always wanted a flower shop. But of course, I should give some to charity." She sighed softly. "After all this time, good fortune has decided to shine upon us."

Dev looked up to see Elodie watching them from across the room. Her eyes were filled with tears. "I think a flower shop would be perfect for you. We haven't had one in town for years. And there's that pretty little storefront on the corner of Maple and Main that's been for sale forever. I bet you could get it for a song."

Mary stood up and tucked the check into her uniform pocket. "I think I'll make a trip to the bank."

"I'll take you, Mom."

"No, no, I'd like to walk. I want to spend some time with this check before I turn it over."

"We should probably keep this to ourselves for now," Dev warned. "I'll call Bob Burnett at the bank and let him know you're coming. Go right to him when you get there."

Mary hugged Dev again. "What are you going to do with your windfall?"

"I'm not sure," Dev said. "Invest it, I suppose."

Mary hurried out of the house, the screen door slamming behind her. Elodie crossed the room and handed him a champagne flute. "I've never seen her so happy."

"Neither have I," Dev said. "She's had such a hard

life. If this money can buy her a little happiness, then I'm forever grateful."

"To Irish ancestors," Elodie said, holding up her glass.

"To DNA tests," Dev countered.

They both drained their champagne flutes, and Elodie refilled them. "You said you were thinking of investing the money. In what?"

"In us," Dev said.

She frowned. "What does that mean?"

"I was talking to Joanie about the meeting last night and she made a good point. If they don't pass your zoning variance, why not consider another spot for the gallery? There are a lot of empty shops downtown. You could even renovate a small part of the factory."

"Both of those take money," Elodie said.

"Which I have. Let me invest in your idea, in this town. You were going to go to New York to find investors. Why not find one here? I can't think of a better use for this money."

Elodie smiled, shaking her head. "I know that a million dollars seems like a lot of money. And it is. But when it comes to a project of this magnitude, a million dollars is just a drop in the bucket. A drop that will evaporate overnight. You can't afford to lose this money. I need to find someone who can. Someone with much deeper pockets."

"It's a start," he said. "I'm not going to take no for an answer."

Elodie wrapped her arms around his neck and

dropped a kiss on his lips. "I'm sure I can persuade you," she teased.

"You can't. My mind is made up."

She ran her fingers down his chest, then slipped them beneath his shirt. "Are you sure? Because I suggest you stop thinking with your mind."

Her palm smoothed across the crotch of his pants, and Dev groaned. "This isn't fair at all."

"Oh, I don't know. You might find it very fair once you've taken off your clothes and crawled into my bed."

"I'm on duty."

"I have two words for you. Lunch break."

"It's nine thirty."

"Breakfast break," she said.

With a low groan, Dev pulled the radio from his belt and called dispatch. "Sally, I'm taking a short break for breakfast."

THE NEXT DAY, Elodie rolled over in the tangled sheets, curling her naked body against Dev's, her arm thrown across his chest. The sun had been up for hours but they'd lingered in bed because Dev had the morning off.

"What time is it?" he asked.

"It's nearly eleven," Elodie said. "We still have a half hour. I can make you some breakfast—or lunch."

"I need to take a shower."

"I like it when you smell of my perfume," she said, resting her chin in his chest. "That way, other women know to stay away."

"Is that what you want? Because there are easier

ways to do that than dousing me in your scent. We could just tell everyone that we're—locked down."

"Locked down?"

"Yeah, Jimmy Joe told me I should lock you down. You know, get things settled. Have an understanding."

"You've been talking to Jimmy about our relationship?"

"Actually, he's been giving me unsolicited advice. He seems to understand an awful lot about women. Although I'm beginning to think that most of his advice comes from the music he listens to. There's also something about putting a ring on it."

"Yes, I've heard that one."

"Beyoncé?"

Elodie nodded. "Let's rule that one out for now, though, shall we?"

Dev pushed up on his elbows. "Why? I don't understand why we can't talk about a future together. A future that may contain diamond rings and wedding plans and children. Why can't we talk about that?"

"Because we've only been together for five weeks."

"We've known each other for years."

"All right. Because I don't trust myself to make the right decisions when it comes to you. You're too…easy."

His expression grew cloudy, and he cursed. "Because we messed around the very first night you were in town?"

"That's not the kind of easy I'm talking about," Elodie said. "Choosing you, to be with you. It's easy because we get along so well. We're perfect for each other. And when we're together we're blissfully happy."

"What's wrong with that? Isn't that the kind of relationship you want?"

"That's the way it was with my parents," she said. "They were infatuated with each other. And then the business went bust and they had to deal with the stress of a family catastrophe. Suddenly, things weren't perfect, and they didn't know how to navigate a crisis. Money had always solved their problems. They ended up hating each other. They don't even speak anymore."

"I used to think that the only thing standing between us was money," Dev said. "And now I realize it's true. Only this time it's my money."

Elodie crawled out of bed and began to search for something to wear. "You are entirely too impatient about getting this 'locked down.'"

"I understand why you can't commit. It would mean committing to living in this town for the rest of your life."

"What about Tasmania? You're not going to take your million and run?" she asked.

"You know I won't."

She bent over the bed and kissed him. "And that's why you are the best man I've ever met."

"Elodie!"

The sound of Mary Cassidy's voice rang through the house, and Dev sat up. "What is my mother doing here?"

"We're going downtown to look at some properties for her shop," Elodie said.

"She's taking you and not me?"

Elodie shrugged. "It's a flower shop. Not really a guy kind of thing."

"Is she coming up here?"

Elodie glanced around the doorjamb. "I'll be right down, Mary." She grabbed a cotton sundress and pulled it over her head, then slipped her feet into a pair of comfortable sandals. She kissed him again, pushing him back onto the bed until he groaned softly. "Get dressed and go down the rear stairs. There's no reason to embarrass your mother with your slutty behavior."

Elodie hurried down the stairs to find Mary waiting for her. She wasn't wearing her usual gray uniform, but had chosen a light floral blouse and trim capri pants. It was as if twenty years had disappeared from her face overnight. "You look lovely," Elodie said.

"Is Devin still here?" she asked.

"Devin?"

"Don't be coy, dear. His car is parked out back. I'm well aware he spends most of his nights here. I hear the gossip around town. Is he still here?"

Elodie heard the kitchen screen door squeak, and she shook her head. "He just went out." A few seconds later, the police cruiser drove past the house and out onto the street. Mary let out a tightly held breath.

"Good. I have something I'd like to discuss with you and I couldn't risk Dev overhearing what I had to say." She glanced around. "We need tea. Or maybe coffee? Which would you prefer?"

"Coffee. Come on, I'll help you get it."

They walked to the kitchen together, and Elodie pulled up a stool for Mary while she put the teakettle on to boil. Then she moved to fill the coffee filter with fresh grounds and water. When that was brewing, she turned back to Mary.

"Is everything all right?"

"No," Mary said. "I have to ask your advice, but when I tell you this story, I fear it will change the way you see me. You may not like me at all. But I'm not sure what to do and you've always been so sensible."

"Tell me this story," Elodie said.

"I'm not sure how much your parents informed you about my past. Or how much Dev may have revealed. Though he doesn't really know a lot of this story, and some of what he believes to be fact isn't exactly the truth. What is true is that my father deserted my mother when I was four years old. She died when I was fifteen and your family took care of me. I worked in their house as a maid while I finished school.

"I worked for your family for seventeen years and when I was thirty-four, I met a man. He was handsome and charming and he swept me off my feet. I ran away with him and I thought our life would be perfect. I'd waited so long for love that I was willing to convince myself of anything."

"Where did you go?" Elodie asked.

"We moved around a lot. This man made his money outside the law. I guess you'd call him a con man. We had Devin and he seemed pleased to be a father. But a year after Devin was born, I got pregnant again and my husband deserted me. I returned to your father's house to ask for my job back. He agreed to rehire me, but as a condition, he strongly suggested I give up my baby for adoption. He and your mother would find a good family and in exchange, he'd provide a house for me and Devin."

Elodie gasped. "My father made you give up your child?"

"He was right. I wasn't prepared to take care of two children and hold down a job on my own. And he promised that my son would be better off. I needed the job, I needed a place to live, so I agreed."

Elodie was stunned. Her first memories of Mary came from when she was five or six years old. She would have been a toddler when all this had happened. Her older brothers would have remembered better. Why had they never mentioned it? Why hadn't Dev— Then she understood. "You never told Dev he had a brother."

Mary shook her head, tears flooding her eyes. "I've always meant to, but the time never seemed right. And now, I can't possibly reveal the truth because he'll never forgive me."

Elodie slid over and put her arm around Mary's shoulders. "And this has come up because of the inheritance? Because this son that you gave away deserves his share, as well?"

Mary nodded. "With the money, I could find him, hire detectives."

"My father would know where he is."

"I couldn't ask him. I promised we'd never speak of it again."

"I could ask. I could make him tell me."

"If we just found out where he was, then I could give

the information to Mr. Stephens and he could send him a check. I'd never have to say anything to Devin."

Elodie took her hand and gave it a squeeze. "Mary, I think he deserves the truth. He has a brother. If it were me, I'd want to know."

"And would you hate me for keeping the secret for so long?"

Elodie shook her head. "I might be angry for a little while. But I'd come to understand eventually."

"Do you really believe your father will reveal where my son went?"

"I'm going to have to pay him a visit. It's not something I can ask over the phone, but yes, I'll get the answer."

Mary gave her a hug, followed by a wavering smile. "Will you be there when I tell Devin?"

"Of course."

"I never had a daughter, but I often thought of you as my own. I was there for most of your childhood. I helped you through the rough teenage years. And when you and Devin found each other all those years ago, I hoped that it would last and that someday, you'd be a part of our family. But if you can't be my daughter, then I'm happy to call you my friend."

Elodie took Mary's hand. "Well, friend, let's go out and see if we can find you a pretty spot for your flower shop."

They decided to walk downtown, enjoying the warm, breezy day. But as they chatted about Mary's plans, Elodie couldn't put aside the revelations that Dev's mother had made. She had no idea how Dev might react. Unlike her, he'd never had cause to question his loyalty to his family.

So many things had been tipped upside down in their lives. What would be next?

9

DEV SAT ON the front steps of the mansion on Wisteria Street. He stared out at a pair of pedestrians walking a small dog and recognized the high school principal and his wife. They waved and he returned the gesture.

"Look at that. Their lives go on, as they have day after day, and they blindly believe that everything is right with the world. And they have no idea that there are volcanoes and missiles and tsunamis just over the horizon."

Elodie rested her head against his shoulder. "I know it's a lot to take in, but I have to say that I admire the way you handled your mother. She was so scared of how you might react to the news."

"I'm the last one to question her choices. She's always put me above everything else. I'm just surprised that she could have given my brother away."

"I suspect my father put a great deal of pressure on her and she didn't have the strength to fight him. He held all the cards—her job, her house, your future."

"I had no idea," he said.

"I wonder what other secrets they're keeping from us," Elodie murmured.

"You think there's something else?"

"I don't know. But I'm going to find out. My father is going to be in New York this weekend. And I need to go back anyway and talk to some potential donors for the gallery. I have a ticket for tomorrow afternoon."

Dev slipped his arm around her shoulders. "I don't want you to go."

She reached out and touched his cheek. "When were you going to tell me about the zoning decision? Mary mentioned that they weren't going to be ruling in my favor and that everyone in town knows about it."

Dev glanced away, shaking his head. "I wasn't going to say anything until I tried to change their minds. Now that I have all this money, I figured a few well-placed bribes might do the trick."

"I hope you're kidding," Elodie said.

"Not at all. I'm pretty sure that's how your father got things done around town."

"Well, you don't have to commit a crime on my behalf. I've decided to sell the house. I've got some buyers interested and I think they'll meet my counteroffer. It's just too much for me to care for, and the mill is probably a better location for the gallery anyway."

"I could always buy it," Dev suggested.

Elodie drew back, sending him a look of disbelief. "What would you do with a house this big?"

"Live in it. Fix it up. If you aren't going to be around, I'll need to have something to do with my spare time."

"Maybe you'll find another girlfriend," Elodie said.

"Is that what you were? Were you my girlfriend?"

Though he'd made his tone light, the questions were serious. Was this how it would end? Would she leave for New York and never return? He was almost afraid to ask about her plan for fear that his interest might drive her away.

She'd given up on the gallery at the mansion, but had she given up on everything else? "Maybe I will," Dev said. "And if I find one, this fancy house will go a long way to impressing her, don't you think?" He paused. "And there is that cold steel countertop on a hot summer night. It's one of my favorite features."

She laughed, but Dev wasn't going to tell her that he wasn't kidding. He didn't want the mansion to be sold to strangers. This was their house—his and Elodie's—and he wanted to build a future here. Maybe she didn't see it yet, but Dev had to have faith that she would sooner or later. It might not be for a week or a month or maybe even a year, but she'd realize that she loved him and she'd be back. He wanted the house to be waiting for them both.

"When do you think you'll be home again?" he asked.

She was silent for a long time. "I can't answer that. If I can't come up with a viable plan for the mill, if I can't convince enough people to invest, then I might never come back. Not to live. I have to be able to make a living here."

"You don't," he said. "You could live with me. We

could use my inheritance to buy a business for you to run."

"That money is yours," she said. "Can you imagine what people would say? A Winchester finds yet another way to steal someone's money. I'll visit. And you'll come to see me. It's not a perfect plan, but we could make it work."

Dev ought to have been satisfied with what she offered. It was better than no contact at all. As long as they still found time to be together, he still had a chance to convince her that life could be good in Winchester.

"What are you going to do? For work?"

"The gallery I used to work for wants to rehire me. And it's decent there. I've got a lot of contacts. If I can find someone who wants to invest in the mill, then I'll come back. It's not like we'll never see each other again. We're adults. There are planes that fly between Asheville and New York. Three hours."

"It won't be the same," he said.

Elodie shook her head. "It won't be. But it will still be good. I promise." She stood up and pulled him to his feet. "Come on. You can keep me company while I pack."

"No," Dev said. "I'm not going to watch you pack. I'd do almost anything to make you happy, but I draw the line at that." He sighed softly. "I almost wish you hadn't come home. I was fine with my life before you showed up. I was relatively happy. I understood where I belonged and I was content. But now, you've changed all of that."

"I know what you want, Dev. And I'd like to believe

that we could live here, happily ever after. But the town has already rejected me. And if we were together, they'd start to hate you, too. This is not the place for us. And I'm not sure where that place would be."

Dev stood up. "I'm going to take a walk."

"I'll come with you," Elodie said.

"No, you have to pack." He bent close and kissed her forehead. "I'll be back, I promise. This might be the last night we spend together in a long time."

The expression on her face betrayed her concern. She didn't think he'd return. In truth, Dev wasn't sure he could. She seemed so casual about leaving, as if it would have no effect at all on their happiness. Dev wanted to grab her and give her a good shake, to shout at her and tell her that she was walking away from something great and wonderful. Something so precious that it didn't come along often.

He pulled her into his arms and gave her a fierce hug. There was so much he wanted to say. But it seemed the harder he tried to convince her, the more she pulled away. She couldn't admit that she needed him. But then, maybe she didn't. He jogged down the front walk and headed downtown, setting a leisurely pace. It was nearly 10:00 p.m. on a weeknight but a cool breeze and full moon had brought people out for late strolls.

He recognized everyone he met on the street. Every name. He knew their families, their professions, their addresses. He knew the names of their dogs and their kids. Dev had made his life about saving the town of Winchester. People had trusted him to have an idea of what was best for the citizens, and he'd served them with honor.

What would happen if someone else took over, someone not so ethical? Everything that he'd accomplished would be destroyed and the town would be left to wither and die like so many other industrial towns.

He walked up and down Main Street, smiling to himself as he thought about his boyhood, when Main Street had bustled with business and there hadn't been an empty storefront to be seen. It could be like that again. He could make it happen.

But now Dev realized that he didn't want to do it alone. He needed Elodie by his side, focused on the same goals and ambitions, there to pick him up when he felt down and to celebrate his successes. Was he being selfish to want her with him? Maybe so, but he had to believe that deep down inside, she wanted the same thing.

As he continued his walk, the streets grew empty and when the midnight bell from the Episcopalian Church rang twelve, he knew it was time to head back to the house.

She'd left the light on and the front door open. He slipped inside and locked the door behind him, then walked through the empty rooms, switching off the lights as he went. Slowly, he climbed the stairs and slipped into her room. The bedside lamp was on, the shade covered by a silk scarf, creating a romantic atmosphere.

She was already asleep, the thin cotton sheet outlining her naked body beneath. Dev stood at the door for a long time, watching her, memorizing every detail of her face until he was certain he could re-create it perfectly in his mind.

She stirred, rolling onto her side and kicking her leg out from beneath the sheets. Dev walked to the bed and sat down on the edge. Reaching out, he brushed a pale tendril of hair away from her temple. He bent close and pressed a kiss to the spot where her hair had been. And when he drew back, her eyes were open.

"You're back," she murmured. "I wasn't sure you'd come."

"I said I would," Dev replied. He stood and slowly stripped off his clothes. She held up the sheet, and he crawled in beside her.

For a long while they didn't speak, just held each other. Finally, Elodie rolled over and braced her arms on his chest, looking at him in the darkened room. Moonlight streaming through the window outlined her profile, and Dev reached out and traced the shape of her mouth with his fingertip.

"I love you," she said. "You need to know that. I've never loved anyone like I love you. But I'm not sure what that means. I wish I could make sense of it because then you wouldn't be so sad."

"I'm not going anywhere," Dev said. "And when you figure it all out, I'll be here, waiting. Or you can call and I'll come to you. Because I love you, Ellie. I have from that first time we spoke at the Christmas party. You were the most interesting, beautiful, clever girl I'd ever met and I knew we were meant to be together. I still believe that."

She leaned forward and kissed him, sweetly at first. But then Dev wrapped his arms around her waist and pulled her beneath him, settling his hips between her legs. This was where he belonged. Wherever she was, that was home to him. Someday, she'd understand and then he'd believe her words of love.

THE RESTAURANT WAS packed with lunchtime diners as Elodie wove her way through the tables. As she approached, her father, Frederick Winchester, stood. His expression was unreadable and she wondered what was going through his head.

She'd never demanded an audience with her father. In the Winchester family, her father was the only one who did the demanding. In truth, she was surprised he'd agreed to come. But then, maybe there were some things that he intended to say. The maître d' pulled out the chair for her, and she leaned forward and kissed her father's cheek before she sat. "Hello, Daddy. You look well."

He was dressed in an impeccably tailored suit and an expensive silk shirt that showed off his tan. He looked remarkably young and vibrant for a man of nearly sixty-five years. Elodie wondered if he might have had some plastic surgery recently.

"I've lost some weight. Your mother took me to court again on her maintenance. I can't afford to eat out as much as I used to."

"It's probably better for you," Elodie said. "At least it's healthier. How is Mom?"

"Fine," he said. "She's dating some golf pro. He's

taught her how to play. Can you imagine your mother out on a golf course, swinging a club? There was a time when she would have considered that type of man beneath her."

"Times change, Daddy. Are you dating anyone?"

Frederick held up his hand, and when the waiter approached, he ordered another martini on the rocks. "What can I get you?"

"Wine," she said to the waiter. "A bottle of your best pinot noir."

"Well, there you go. Let's you and I spend the afternoon getting ourselves thoroughly pissed." He took a long drink of his martini, then popped the olive in his mouth. "You look good. Got a bit of sun. Have you been on vacation?"

"Actually, I've spent the last couple of months in Winchester."

At first, her father seemed stunned. Then, he laughed. "Why would you spend a minute of your time in that place?"

"You forget, I got the house in the settlement. I'm trying to figure out what to do with it."

"And what have you decided?"

"I'm going to sell it. But the mill is also still on the market. The bank owns that. It's a shame, really, because it would make a great retail space. Carved up into shops and workshops it could be quite nice."

"Who in that town can afford to shop?"

"No one," she said. "Thanks to you and my brothers. But things are changing. Slowly."

"You're wasting your time, Ellie, no matter what

you're doing in that town." Her father studied her for a long moment. "Wait. Don't tell me. You've hooked up with that punk. That Cassidy kid. Is that why you went?"

Elodie took a slow sip of her wine. "He's not a kid anymore, Daddy. He's a full-grown man. And still as wonderful as he always was."

"He's beneath you, Elodie. He always has been, always will be. You deserve someone who can make your life comfortable, not some townie."

"Rather than someone who can make my life happy?" She smiled wryly. "How did being 'comfortable' work out for you? Did you hear that Mary and Dev Cassidy are both wealthier than you are now? Huge inheritance from a lost aunt in Ireland. It was quite the news around town."

"Well, well. Maybe he can lend me a few thousand."

"After what you took away from him, I doubt that will be happening."

Her father studied her for a long moment. "What are you talking about?"

"Mary's baby. Devin Cassidy's younger brother."

"Mary agreed never to talk about that. But then, I suppose she doesn't have a reason to keep her secrets anymore."

"Where is he? You arranged for the adoption. Who did you give him to?"

"I don't have to tell you that," he said.

"Yes, you do. At some point in your life, you're going to need to start making restitution for what you did to the people of Winchester. This would be a good start.

Do it for Mary, who did nothing but love and care for your family for decades."

Frederick took a sip of his drink, then studied a spot near the center of the table. She watched her father breathing in and out, and Elodie cursed inwardly. He wasn't going to tell her.

"Cooper. Judge Benjamin Cooper. He was the sitting judge in a lawsuit brought against Winchester Mills. We could have lost millions. I got his wife the baby she always wanted and he got rid of our lawsuit."

"Do you have any idea where he is now?"

"No. He left Winchester a few years after that. I think they were afraid Mary might recognize her child once he grew up."

The waiter appeared at the table to take their lunch order, but now that she'd secured the information she needed, Elodie didn't see the point of staying. "I'm really not hungry, Daddy."

"Sit," he said.

"I have to—"

"Sit down, Elodie. You're going to have lunch with me and we're going to chat like normal people do. Then you can leave. I won't even make you eat dessert."

Reluctantly, she sat down. They used to have such a wonderful relationship, Elodie mused. She used to worship her father. And then, he'd sent her away and everything had changed. She'd never been able to trust him after that.

Her father had dictated the terms of Elodie's life. Her father had bullied her and berated her and dismissed her, all for falling in love as any teenager would. And she'd sworn to herself that she'd never again allow anyone to control her life.

She slowly sat down, then poured herself another glass of wine. "We'll need a few more minutes," she told the waiter.

Was that why she was so reluctant to commit to Dev? Was she afraid that he would expect the same control over her life as her father had?

"You're going to sell the house," her father stated.

"I was going to try to turn it into a gallery, but I couldn't get a variance on the zoning laws."

Frederick chuckled. "That's kind of ironic. I wrote those zoning laws."

"But if I can find someone to invest in the mill, we might be able to transform it into small shops and workspaces, and maybe even apartments for artists. If we can create an artists' colony in Winchester, we may be able to bring in tourists, too."

"I can see this means something to you, and contrary to what you believe, I do love you, Elodie. It's obvious I can't keep you from that boy. So I'll give you some insider information if you promise not to say where you got it," her father said. He leaned in. "Next April, they're going to break ground on a new championship golf course about seven miles out of town. Thirty-six holes, plus a small resort and spa. And there are plans to add another thirty-six holes within the next ten years."

"How do you know this?"

"I still have some contacts in the area. They called to see if I wanted to invest. They didn't realize I was broke. But I guess the news was worth something after all."

"Who else is aware of this?"

"That, I can't say. But if you're looking for someone to invest in your little project, call Avery James here in New York. It's the kind of project he likes. And he probably already invested in the golf course."

"Thank you, Daddy. It's good information."

"I'm still good for a few things," he said, his words dripping with sarcasm. He waved down the waiter for another drink, and the waiter took their order.

"So are you in love with the punk?" Frederick asked.

"He's not a punk. He's the police chief in Winchester now."

"Police chief? A government job. You can't beat that."

"Stop," she said. "You aren't allowed to speak badly of him. Not after what you did. He's a good man. And he cares for me. And I'd be lucky if we ended up together."

"But you don't love him."

"I do," she said. "I always have. I've tried to convince myself that I couldn't possibly have met the man of my dreams when I was twelve years old, but I think I did."

"You always idolized him," her father said. "We suspected it might be a problem, and when it started to seem likely that you'd end up pregnant as a teenager, we sent you away. We protected you from him. From making a mistake that you couldn't fix. I'll never regret that. Look at you. You have all the choices in the world now."

"And if I choose him?" Elodie asked.

"There's nothing I can do about that," Frederick said. "But I suppose if he's the one you really want, then you should marry him. Don't waste any more time. You're nearly thirty. You don't want to wait much longer to have children, do you?"

"Daddy, stop giving me advice. I can run my own life."

He chuckled. "Yes, I guess you can. So, if we can't talk about your life and what I think you should be doing with it, what can we talk about?"

"How about who else you suspect might be willing to invest…"

"SIGN HERE, HERE AND HERE."

Dev scribbled his name next to the small stickers, then moved on to the next sheaf of papers.

"Here and here," the broker added.

When they'd gone through every last document, the real estate broker placed all the documents into a folder and handed Dev an envelope.

"Well, this has been a most unusual sale, Mr. Cassidy. You coming in at the last minute with an offer made for quite a bit of tension. But you have the house you wanted and for a decent price, I might add."

"I would have paid more," Dev said with a grin.

"I expect you would have," she said. "But you can use that money to renovate. You're taking on a huge project."

Dev opened the envelope to find a familiar set of keys. He ran his fingers over them, remembering the last time he'd seen them in Elodie's hand.

"There is one thing. I don't want you to let Elodie know who bought the house. If she asks, just say it was the couple from the city, the couple who made the first offer."

"Why don't you want her to know?"

"I have my reasons. I'm just going to need some time."

"It will be published in the local papers," she said.

"Elodie doesn't read the local papers," he said.

"All right. I'll do my best."

Dev got up from the conference table. "I'd appreciate that." He tossed the keys in the air, then shoved them in his pocket. "By the way, I've been thinking I might hire a decorator. Can you recommend anyone?"

"Interior designer," the broker said. "That's what they're called. And yes, I can give you a few names."

"Good. I want the house done by Christmas."

"Have you ever renovated a house, Mr. Cassidy?"

He shook his head. "I've never owned a house."

"You're in for a good time," she said. "Just remember, whatever they say it's going to cost, double it. And however long they say it's going to take, double it. Just double everything."

"Good advice," Dev said.

Dev walked back to his car and slid in behind the wheel. He drew a deep breath and closed his eyes. Buying the house had been a leap of faith, but now that it was officially his, there seemed to be a certain logic to it all. Once a sign of power and wealth in the community, now the old Winchester mansion was owned by an ordinary guy. Sure, he was technically a millionaire, at least until he'd written the check for the house.

The closing for the house had taken place at the bank

in town, and it was a short drive to Elodie's place. He stopped short. "Elodie's place," he murmured. He'd always think of it as her house. But maybe, if things turned out right, he could start to think of it as their house.

She'd been gone for a week and his life had reverted back to what it had been before she'd arrived. His days were taken up with work and his evenings with activities that did nothing to alleviate the boredom of living in Winchester.

They'd talked every night via video chat on his office computer, and it was almost like having her with him. Though he couldn't touch her or kiss her, he could still look at her beautiful face and imagine how good it would be the next time they were together.

As he drove toward Wisteria Street, his cell phone rang. He turned it on, recognizing Elodie's number. "Hello," he said. "This is a nice surprise."

"I just had to call," she said. "The real estate broker just phoned. She closed on the sale of the house today. I guess the couple decided on a cash-only deal and wanted to move up their closing date."

"That's great," he said.

"I wanted to let you know."

"Why is that?" Dev asked.

"Because…" She paused for a long moment, the line going silent.

"Because you'd hoped that one day you and I would live in that house?" Dev asked.

"Yes," she said.

"So, I guess I shouldn't count on that."

"No, you shouldn't."

"Can I count on you?"

"You know you can."

Dev pulled up in front of the mansion and shut the car off. "I was considering grabbing a few vacation days at the end of this week. I could fly up to New York and we could spend some time together."

"Not this weekend," she said. "I have a couple of meetings up in Boston and then I have to fly to California on Sunday night."

"For how long?"

"Three days," she said.

"I could always fly out there."

She grew silent again, and Dev scolded himself inwardly for pushing her so hard. "Never mind. I forgot, I have to go to a conference on Monday in Winston-Salem so I wouldn't be able to come anyway."

"You don't have to play games with me," she murmured.

"I'm not," Dev said. "It's just hard to know how to react. We don't do well over the phone." He paused. "Promise me something, will you?"

"Sure," Elodie said.

"If you ever pick up your phone, or your computer, and you feel the least bit reluctant or unhappy or bothered to have to talk to me, you just stop calling. I'll understand."

"That's not going to happen," Elodie said.

"I hope you're right." He swallowed hard. "I have to go. I'll talk to you later. Or maybe I won't."

Dev switched off the phone, cursing softly. How

much longer could they go on like this? The intimacy that they'd found together was beginning to unravel and there were moments when it felt as if he were talking to a stranger. She wasn't the sweet, playful small-town girl that he'd fallen in love with. Instead, she was cool…sophisticated…aloof.

He didn't want to fight with her, especially over the phone, but every time they talked he felt her slipping away and he'd wanted to say something. As far as he was concerned, the choice was simple. She loved him or she didn't. There was no in between.

He glanced at the house, staring at his latest purchase. Either it would turn out to be the biggest mistake he'd ever made or the most brilliant move of his life.

A rap on the driver's side window startled him out of his thoughts. Dev glanced up and found his mother standing on the street next to the car. He rolled down the window. "Hi, Mom."

"You have to stop this, Devin. She's not here anymore. The house is sold. You can't keep mooning around after her. It won't bring her back."

"That's not it, Mom," he murmured. "And what are you doing here?"

"I told Elodie that I'd try to get a look at the new owners and see what they were like."

"And then you're supposed to call her?"

Mary nodded. "She's just curious if they have children and what they do for a living. I'm hoping they stop by. I thought I might introduce myself and mention that I used to be a housekeeper in the mansion, and if they have any questions, they can call me."

"You sound like a stalker," Dev said. "And I should have you arrested."

"You won't," Mary said.

"No. But you don't have to talk to them. I know all about the new owner. There are no children. Just a single guy."

"I heard it was a couple," Mary said.

"Nope. Single guy. Handsome. Rich. Very, very smart. Extremely brilliant, I'd say"

"You've met him?"

Dev reached into his pocket and grabbed the keys, then dangled them out the window. "So, want to walk through my new house with me?"

"You bought her house?"

"I'm thinking of it as *our* house."

Mary laughed. "You are optimistic."

"I had a very good teacher," Dev said.

ELODIE HAD FLOWN into Asheville the night before and had stayed hidden away in the hotel there. She'd been just a few miles away from Dev, and it had taken all her willpower to keep herself from driving into Winchester and surprising him.

It had been nearly six weeks since they'd seen each other, and Elodie couldn't stand it anymore. It had become so difficult to pretend that phone calls and video chats were enough. She craved physical contact. She found herself daydreaming about his hands and his fingers, his lips and his tongue and what he'd been able to do to her body when given the chance.

She'd replayed nearly every minute of their time together in her head, trying to figure out what it was that had made it so wonderful. In the end, Elodie was forced to admit that she'd been madly in love with Dev and that none of her feelings had disappeared since they'd left each other. And after talking with her father, she'd realized that Dev was nothing like Frederick Winchester. He'd never tried to control her, he'd always respected her wishes. He'd always believed in them—she'd been the coward.

But she'd needed the distance to realize what it all meant. She'd been too close to him to see what they had for what it was. Not just desire or lust or passion. But real and true and deep love. Love that could last a lifetime.

The moment she finally figured it out, Elodie booked her ticket home. She was going home to the man she loved. And with every minute that passed, she worried that she may have messed it up. Had his feelings diminished over their time apart? Had he met someone else?

She had the whole evening planned out in her head. She'd called Mary to make sure Dev didn't have any plans. She'd go to his apartment and make a video call on her cell phone, pretending to be in Manhattan. She'd tease him, seduce him over the phone until he was desperate for her. And then she'd knock on his door and let the evening take its usual course. Sex, more sex, and then maybe some dinner. And then hours and hours of even more sex.

As she made the early afternoon drive into Winchester, she grabbed her phone and rechecked her appointment with the agent from the bank. She was scheduled to meet with an associate from Avery James's office to show him the old mill and to discuss her plans for renovating it.

Avery James had agreed to explore the possibility. They'd start by having his architects examine the building. If it looked sound, they'd proceed with drawings and plans and meetings with the bank. But even if her plans for the mill fell apart, she'd find some way to make her idea work. Because Winchester was her home, and always would be.

Elodie hoped she'd be able to sneak into town without Dev finding out. He did have a knack for knowing when something odd was happening in Winchester. But she was betting on Mary being able to keep her visit quiet.

The old mill stood on a vast piece of property right next to the river. Made from stone milled from the mountains, it stood like a silent sentinel over the town, its windows dark, walls stained with soot.

Elodie had spent hours of her childhood at the mill. Her father used to pay her a quarter to sweep up the cotton dust that had gathered into little bunnies on the edges of the vast loom rooms. She found the door open and walked inside, calling out as the door creaked.

"Hello?"

"Miss Winchester?"

"Yes," she said.

"I'm Sophia Markesan from the bank. The electricity is off, so there are no lights. But the windows are big and it's a sunny day. Is it just you?"

"No, I'm meeting someone. His name is—"

"Hello!" A deep voice drifted in from the door, and they both turned to see a younger man enter. He held out his hand. "I'm Jeff Dupree, Avery James's associate."

Elodie made the introductions, then took the keys from Sophia and told her she'd drop them off at the bank when they were done. When she rejoined Jeff, he was anxious to explore the rest of the building.

"I've never been inside a fabric mill before," he said. "When was this built?"

"Between 1882 and 1897," she said. "This building closest to the river is the oldest."

"So the mill used water power?"

"Early on, in the 1700s, they were run with water power. But these mills were first powered by steam," Elodie said. "And later electricity. But with steam came the constant threat of fire, so you needed a source of water to fight a fire, and that's why they were built alongside the river."

They walked through the offices and then up the stairs into the loom room. She drew the doors back, the old iron rollers groaning as the plank door slid to the right.

"Wow," Jeff said. "This is huge."

"It had to be," Elodie explained.

"This has got to be a hundred yards long. And completely open."

"I think it's about two hundred and fifty feet. And it's solidly built. These are timber beams and a plank floor that held tons of equipment. It's overbuilt for what we'd use it for."

"You don't have to convince me, Miss Winchester. I see the possibilities."

"Then you like it?"

"I do," he said. "I'd love to do a project in this space."

Elodie smiled and clapped her hands. "Really?"

"Really. That doesn't mean it's a done deal, but I'm impressed enough that I'll start looking at some plans. The price is certainly right. And with the new golf resort going in, it would be the perfect time. One thing you should do, however, if you want to make this an artists' colony, is line up some corporate sponsors for the artists. If we can rent out fifty percent of our shops and studios by the time we're done with renovation, it will go a long way to getting the project approved."

"I can do that." She threw her arms around Jeff and gave him a quick hug. But the gesture of gratitude was interrupted by a familiar voice.

"Elodie?"

She drew back and turned around to find Dev standing in the doorway. Her heart skipped, and she wanted to run to him and launch herself into his arms. "Dev. What are you doing here?"

"I got a call that there were people inside the mill."

"This is Jeff Dupree from Avery James and Associates. He's an architect. His firm might be interested in helping me with the mill project."

"Why didn't you tell me you were coming into town?"

She turned to Jeff. "Can you excuse me for a moment? Just go ahead and look around."

She followed Dev out into the stairwell and the moment they were out of sight, he grabbed her and covered her mouth with his like a man desperate for the taste of her lips. He pushed her back against the wall. Grabbing her wrists, he pinned them above her head. Elodie arched her body against his, their hips meeting in an erotic dance.

When he finally drew away, she was breathless. But Elodie grabbed the front of his shirt and pulled him into another mind-numbing kiss.

"I can't believe you're here," he murmured, his lips hot against her throat.

"And I can't believe you messed up my big surprise. I had it all planned out. I even called your mother."

"I can always pretend I didn't see you here," Dev said. "When are you finished?"

"This is probably going to take at least an hour. Maybe two," she said. "I can stop by the station when I'm done."

He nodded. "All right. There's something I want to show you, actually." Dev pulled her into another kiss. "I don't want to let you go," he whispered. "I'm afraid you might disappear."

"Don't worry," Elodie said. "I'm home now."

Dev stepped back and stared down into her eyes. "You are?"

"I am."

"I'm glad to hear that."

Elodie watched as he walked out, smiling to herself. She'd had a different reunion planned, but this one had turned out perfectly. If she'd had any questions about his affections, they'd been answered immediately. All that was left was to tell him that he'd been right all along—that she belonged here in Winchester with him.

She hurried back to Jeff, dust motes flying up around her shoes as she moved. She found him at the far end of the adjacent room, his jacket off, his tie undone, an old ladder braced against one of the timber cross beams.

"I just wanted to get a picture of these joints here. They're amazing. This place could withstand any force of nature—except a fire, maybe. It's been built for strength." He crawled down the ladder. "Amazing."

"I'm so glad you're enthusiastic about the mill and this project."

"And I can't tell you how happy we are that you brought it to us. Mr. James has authorized me to make you a partner in this project. We'd like you to work for us. You know the town, the history of this building. It would be wonderful to have a Winchester on board. You'd have an office in our New York location, but you'd be spending a few weeks down here each month until construction begins. Then, we'd expect you to move down here full-time."

"A job," she said. "That would be great. I want to see this project through."

"Good. I can tell Mr. Avery that you're on board."

"Not yet," she said. "There are a few things I need to work out first."

"What might those things be?" Jeff asked.

"Personal things," she said. "About where I'm meant to live—here or New York."

DEV PACED THE length of his office, glancing at his watch every few minutes. It had been two hours. She ought to have been here by now. He fought the impulse to go back to the mill and see what was taking so long.

The buzzer sounded on his phone, and he pushed the intercom button.

"Elodie Winchester is here," Sally said.

"Thanks, I'll be right out." He drew a deep breath, knowing that another greeting like the one he'd given her at the mill would have to be delayed until they got out to the car.

He found her in the lobby, chatting with Sally and Kyle as if they were old friends. She met his gaze as he crossed the room, a smile twitching at the corners of her lips. When he reached her, he bent close and brushed a kiss to her cheek. "Hey there."

"Hello," Elodie said.

"Have you had lunch?" Dev asked.

"I haven't. I had a late breakfast at the hotel in Asheville, but just toast and some fruit."

"Let's go," he said. "Sally, I'm on lunch."

"Got it, boss," she said with a wide smile.

They walked out into the late afternoon sunshine. "Are you finished with your work for the day?" Dev asked.

She nodded.

"How did it go?"

"I'm so excited," she said. "Jeff loves the idea, and with the new golf resort going in outside town, there's—"

"Golf resort?"

"That's supposed to be secret," she said. "So don't tell anyone. I think they're still trying to put the land deal together. But a developer is planning a seventy-two-hole resort with a hotel and spa."

"Can you imagine what that would do for the town? The number of jobs alone could change the whole outlook here in Winchester."

"And they believe that once the resort is built, there will be a need for tourist shops here in town, and that the mill would be a perfect place to develop. Of course, some shops will still be located on Main Street, but both places will benefit."

When they reached the car, Dev slipped his hands around her waist and pulled her into a deep and lingering kiss. Pressing his forehead against hers, he smiled. "I can't seem to stop myself from kissing you."

"So my surprise had the intended effect?"

"Can't you tell?" he asked.

Her stomach growled, and Elodie laughed. "I guess I'm hungrier than I thought. Where are we going to eat?"

"We could go down to Zelda's," he said. "But there's a new place I want to show you."

"A new place in Winchester? That's a good thing."

He helped her into the car, and they drove toward the Winchester mansion. When he pulled up in front of it, she glanced over at him, frowning. "Here?"

Dev nodded. "You'll love it."

"I didn't know the new buyers planned to open a restaurant. Wouldn't that require a commercial variance? How could the council give one to the new owners and not me?"

"It's a very exclusive restaurant. And it's not really

a restaurant but an eating experience. Does that make sense?"

She gave him a confused look. "No. What are you babbling about?"

"Don't worry. I'm sure you'll love it."

"Do we need a reservation?" she asked.

"No, we can just walk in. I know the owner really well." He tucked her hand in the crook of his arm and walked up the front walk, trying to keep himself from grinning.

"New roof," she said. "And fresh paint on the porch. Those baskets of flowers are so beautiful. They've gotten a lot of work done in six weeks."

"You should see the inside." He held the door open for her, and Elodie stepped into the hall. A soft gasp slipped from her lips as she took in the finely decorated interior. "What do you think?"

"It's lovely," she said. She walked to a sideboard and ran her hand over it. "Elegant, but not fussy." She looked down at the floors. "These rugs are gorgeous. And the floors have been refinished. It's like a brand-new house."

"Nice enough for you to live in?"

"Who wouldn't want to live here? I wonder what they did with my room."

"Would you like to find out?"

"We can't just wander through the house uninvited. Shouldn't we ask the owner?"

He slipped his hands around her waist. "Sure. Go ahead and ask me."

"Ask you? But—"

"Yes. Say, 'Can I see more of the house, please?'"

"Can I see—" The words died in her throat. "Did you buy this house, Dev?"

He nodded. "I did."

The expression on her face was pure shock at first. But then, a smile touched her lips and it grew to a huge grin. "You bought the house."

"For us," he said. "We can't live in my apartment. And this place was comfortable for both of us. I couldn't imagine living anywhere else."

"But you didn't even know if I was coming back. What if I had stayed in New York?"

"I would have had a lot of extra room." He grabbed her hand. "Let me show you the kitchen."

When he pushed open the door, she stepped inside. It had been completely updated. He'd kept all the old cabinets, but had them refinished and fitted with new nickel-plated hardware. And the island had been transformed, the battered stainless steel replaced with granite.

Elodie smoothed her hands over the surface. "It's very cool. Nice for those hot summer nights." She walked around, looking in the oven and running water from the new faucet. "You did this all yourself?"

"I had a decorator here for about a week, but we didn't see eye to eye. So my mom helped me out. She has a good memory for what was in the house when your family lived there." He took her hand and pressed it to his heart.

"There are a lot of things we will still need to do, and anything you don't like, we'll replace. There's a very generous return policy on almost everything I bought. I want this to be our house, Ellie. I want you to live here with me and let me be a part of your life. I couldn't care less if we get married. I just want you in my life, every day."

"I want that, too," Elodie said, running her fingers through the hair at his nape. "I've missed you so much. And I finally realize that this is where I belong. But—"

"But?" he said. "I don't like that word."

"If Avery goes ahead with the mill project, they want me to work with them. In New York, at first. But when construction begins, I'd move down here. It would mean a lot of back-and-forth for about six months to a year, and a delay in my plan to move back here for good. But I'd love to follow through on the project."

"Ellie, you need to be a part of this project. And if I have to wait for you, I'm sure I can do that. It will give me time to finish the second floor."

She threw herself into his arms and gave him a fierce hug. "I knew there was a reason I loved you." She pulled back and met his gaze. "I do love you, Dev."

"And I love you, Ellie."

"We're perfect for each other, aren't we?"

Dev nodded. "We are." He bent close and kissed her. "There is one other thing I have to show you. I think you'll like it."

"I like everything I've seen so far. Please tell me it involves taking your clothes off."

"No. It's up on the third floor."

They took the servants' stairs up to the top story of the house. Dev opened the door that led to what they'd once called the ballroom.

"It's dark up here," Elodie said. "Can you turn on the light?"

"I will. Just go to the top of the stairs and enter the room on your right."

Elodie did as she was told, and when she'd opened the door Dev flipped the lights on. The minute he did, the model trains began to run, circling the tracks as they had all those years ago.

"Oh, my God." She turned and stared at him, complete surprise etched across her face. "How did you do this?"

"The whole set was sold at the bankruptcy auction. I found the guy who'd bought it and asked if he wanted to sell it back to me. He helped me put it together again and now it's where it belongs."

"Do you remember that night?" Elodie asked. "The night I brought you up here? I thought you were the most interesting boy I'd ever met. I decided to marry you that night and so many nights after that."

"I'm hoping you still want to marry me," Dev said. "Because I already went out and bought the ring. I don't want to give it to you until you're ready but—"

"Can I see it?" Elodie asked.

Dev reached in his pocket and held out the box. Elodie took it from him and opened the lid. Her breath caught at the sight and tears filled her eyes. "I recognize this ring. It belonged to my grandmother. She promised it to me, but they had to sell it." Elodie looked up at him and Dev reached out and brushed a tear from her cheek. "How did you do this? How did you know?"

"My mother told me about it. About what it meant to you. It wasn't hard to track it down."

"Ask me," Elodie said, handing him the ring.

"You're sure?"

She nodded, then motioned to the floor. "On one knee."

Dev knelt down in front of her and held out the ring. "Elodie Winchester, I've loved you for nearly my entire life. I can't imagine living another day without you. Will you marry me?"

Elodie nodded. "I will."

He rose and slipped the ring on her finger, then kissed her. He'd never tasted anything as sweet and as perfect. And as he held her close, Dev realized that all the very best things in life were worth waiting for— even if it took eleven years, ten months, four days and six hours.

Epilogue

AILEEN QUINN SAT at her desk, the surface cluttered with photographs. A fire crackled in the hearth, warming the evening chill from the room. Even in the summertime, she felt the damp, making her bones and joints ache with age. The one thing she'd never expected about getting old was that her body would fail her before her mind did. Inside, she still felt like a young woman with years of life ahead of her.

She stared down at the assortment of photos, young people smiling, and remembered the occasion at which each was taken. Many of them were snapped right here at her house in the Irish countryside. Others at important life events—weddings, baptisms, birthday celebrations.

Just a few years ago, she'd been all alone in the world, an orphan without any family left. But when she discovered her family, torn apart by her parents' deaths, she began to collect the pieces of her family, spread all over the world, and put them back together again.

She'd never thought there would be so many, or

that even now, there were more to be found. Her four brothers, boys she'd never known, had carried on the family name in Australia, Canada, New Zealand and the United States, as well as here in Ireland. And now, another had been found—Mary Cassidy and her son, Devin.

She withdrew the letter from its envelope and read the greetings she'd received along with the excitement and gratitude over the inheritance. She'd worked hard for her money, but giving it away to her family members had brought more joy to her than to them.

"What are you doing in here?"

Aileen looked up to see her friend and researcher, Ian Stephens, standing in the doorway of the library. "I'm just going through all these photos. We really should put this in an album or a book of some kind, don't you think?"

Ian crossed to the desk and looked over her shoulder. "I suppose a book would be nice."

"Why don't you write a book about the search? I'm sure people would be interested in reading that."

"We should write a book. But how can we write a book when we never seem to finish this job? Sooner or later, you're going to have to run out of relatives."

"Or money," she said. "Although, I don't think that will be a problem." Aileen held out the newest photo. "Tell me about these two—Mary and Devin."

Ian sat down across from her, settling into one of the comfortable wing chairs, as he related how Lochlan Quinn ended up in the small mill town of Winchester, North Carolina.

"Do you know where Lochlan is buried?" Aileen asked.

"No. But if he died in the US, we should be able to track him. There's always a paper trail, a death certificate, a newspaper obituary. He didn't stay with Mary's mother, and they weren't legally married. He'd left his first wife, then took up with Dierdre O'Meara, Dex and Claire's grandmother. Then he ended up marrying again in the US before disappearing for good."

"So your wife is connected with this family?"

"They share the same grandfather, so that makes them first cousins."

"I suppose we should assume there are more," Aileen said.

"There is at least one," Ian said.

"Do you have a photo?"

"It's a rather tragic story. Mary had a second son after Devin. She gave him up for adoption and he was adopted by Judge Benjamin Cooper and his wife. When the boy was three, his parents were killed in an auto wreck and he was put up for adoption again. And there, we lose track of him."

"You found Devin and Mary and Lochlan in North Carolina," Aileen said. "I trust you'll be able to find this boy. Do we know his name?"

"The Coopers named him Spencer, but his name could have changed again. I haven't been able to find out for sure."

"I guess you'll be off on another adventure then," Aileen said. "I am sorry this has turned into such an endless project."

"No," Ian said. "I'm actually going to miss it once it's over. It's a lot of fun, giving away your money. I like making people happy." He stood. "Claire has come with me and she's brought the children. They're anxious to see their aunt Aileen."

"It's biscuit time," she said. "My very favorite time of day."

Ian left the room, and Aileen slowly got to her feet, reaching for her cane. With all the babies being born into the family, she'd been feeling much younger than her years. In truth, she felt as if she had enough energy to live another lifetime.

"If only they'd issue me a brand-new body," she murmured to herself.

In truth, she'd enjoyed her life and when it finally came to an end, she could close her eyes and know that she'd been happy. And that was all anyone could ask for, wasn't it?

* * * * *

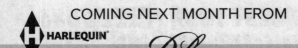
#859 A SEAL'S TEMPTATION
Uniformly Hot!
by Tawny Weber
Lark Sommers is too busy guarding her independence to admit she needs love. Navy SEAL Shane O'Brian is too busy protecting others to realize he yearns for a woman's touch. But the passion between them is about to ignite!

#860 ONE BREATHLESS NIGHT
Three Wicked Nights
by Jo Leigh
On New Year's Eve Rick Sinclair looks like danger and sex wrapped in a tux. Already engaged teacher Jenna Delaney is about to find out if he can teach *her* a few things.

#861 THIS KISS
Made in Montana
by Debbi Rawlins
Ethan Styles is the hottest bull rider on the circuit, but he doesn't stand a chance against one very sexy bounty hunter determined to give him the ride of his life!

#862 INSATIABLE
Unrated!
by Leslie Kelly
A favor from a handsome stranger turns into an insatiable affair that Viv Callahan doesn't want to end. Until she discovers that Damian Black is a tycoon...and that's not his only secret.

HBCNM0815

REQUEST YOUR FREE BOOKS!
2 FREE NOVELS PLUS 2 FREE GIFTS!

HARLEQUIN®

Blaze

red-hot reads!

YES! Please send me 2 FREE Harlequin® Blaze® novels and my 2 FREE gifts (gifts are worth about $10). After receiving them, if I don't wish to receive any more books, I can return the shipping statement marked "cancel." If I don't cancel, I will receive 4 brand-new novels every month and be billed just $4.74 per book in the U.S. or $5.21 per book in Canada. That's a savings of at least 14% off the cover price. It's quite a bargain. Shipping and handling is just 50¢ per book in the U.S. and 75¢ per book in Canada.* I understand that accepting the 2 free books and gifts places me under no obligation to buy anything. I can always return a shipment and cancel at any time. Even if I never buy another book, the two free books and gifts are mine to keep forever.

150/350 HDN GH2D

Name	(PLEASE PRINT)

Address	Apt. #

City	State/Prov.	Zip/Postal Code

Signature (if under 18, a parent or guardian must sign)

Mail to the **Reader Service:**
IN U.S.A.: P.O. Box 1867, Buffalo, NY 14240-1867
IN CANADA: P.O. Box 609, Fort Erie, Ontario L2A 5X3

Want to try two free books from another line?
Call 1-800-873-8635 or visit www.ReaderService.com.

* Terms and prices subject to change without notice. Prices do not include applicable taxes. Sales tax applicable in N.Y. Canadian residents will be charged applicable taxes. Offer not valid in Quebec. This offer is limited to one order per household. Not valid for current subscribers to Harlequin Blaze books. All orders subject to credit approval. Credit or debit balances in a customer's account(s) may be offset by any other outstanding balance owed by or to the customer. Please allow 4 to 6 weeks for delivery. Offer available while quantities last.

Your Privacy—The Reader Service is committed to protecting your privacy. Our Privacy Policy is available online at www.ReaderService.com or upon request from the Reader Service.

We make a portion of our mailing list available to reputable third parties that offer products we believe may interest you. If you prefer that we not exchange your name with third parties, or if you wish to clarify or modify your communication preferences, please visit us at www.ReaderService.com/consumerschoice or write to us at Reader Service Preference Service, P.O. Box 9062, Buffalo, NY 14240-9062. Include your complete name and address.

"I can do almost anything with clay. Pottery is my passion, but I really enjoy sculpting, too. Hang on." Lark smiled and held up one finger, as if Shane would leave the minute she turned around.

She swept into the storage room and bent low to get something from the bottom shelf. And Shane knew it'd take an explosion to get him to move.

Because that was one sweet view.

He watched the way the fabric of her dress sort of floated over what looked to be a Grade A ass, then had to shove his hands into his pockets to hide his reaction.

As Lark came back with something in her hand, she gave him a smile that carried a hint of embarrassment, but unless she could read his mind, he didn't know what she had to be embarrassed about.

"You might like this," she said quietly, wetting her lips before holding out her hand, palm up.

On it was a small, whimsical dragon. Wings unfurled, it looked as if it was smiling.

"You made this?" Awed at the way the colors bled from red to gold to purple, he rubbed one finger over the tiny, detailed scales of the dragon's back. "It's great."

"He's a guardian dragon," Lark said, touching her finger to the cool ceramic, close enough that all he'd have to do was shift his hand to touch her. "You might like one of your own. I can tell Sara worries about you."

Shane grimaced at the idea of his baby sister telling people—especially sexy female people with eyes like midnight—that he needed protecting. Better to change the subject than comment on that.

"It takes a lot of talent to make something this intricate," he said, waiting until her gaze met his to slide his hand over hers. He felt her fingers tremble even as he saw that spark heat. Her lips looked so soft as she puffed out a soft breath before tugging that full bottom cushion between her teeth. He wanted to do that for her, just nibble there for a little while.

"I'm good with my hands," she finally said, her words so low they were almost a whisper.

How good? he wanted to ask, just before he dared her to prove it.

Don't miss
A SEAL'S TEMPTATION by Tawny Weber.
Available in September 2015 wherever
Harlequin® Blaze® books and ebooks are sold.

www.Harlequin.com

Love the Harlequin book you just read?

Your opinion matters.

Review this book on your favorite book site, review site, blog or your own social media properties and share your opinion with other readers!

Be sure to connect with us at:
Harlequin.com/Newsletters
Facebook.com/HarlequinBooks
Twitter.com/HarlequinBooks

JUST CAN'T GET ENOUGH?

Join our social communities
and talk to us online.

You will have access to the latest
news on upcoming titles and special
promotions, but most importantly,
you can talk to other fans about your
favorite Harlequin reads.

Harlequin.com/Community

Facebook.com/HarlequinBooks

Twitter.com/HarlequinBooks

Pinterest.com/HarlequinBooks

THE WORLD IS BETTER WITH

Romance

Harlequin has everything from contemporary, passionate and heartwarming to suspenseful and inspirational stories.

Whatever your mood, we have a romance just for you!

Connect with us to find your next great read, special offers and more.